May 2014

**Modern Jewish Literature
and Culture**
Robert A. Mandel,
series editor

For Stephen
Deborah,
with affection

Selected Praise for John J. Clayton's Fiction

Mitzvah Man

What Clayton demonstrates powerfully in the course of his novel is that un-likely events are likely to occur when a man puts himself in God's hands. That is more than enough to sustain this wise and deeply satisfying novel.

—*Commentary Magazine*

Until now, Clayton has been known for his short stories. If there's any justice, *Mitzvah Man*, his fourth novel, should be his breakout novel. It is that good.

—*Hadassah Magazine*

Pow! . . . Zowee! . . . Whoosh! *Mitzvah Man* is the new-look superhero for the modern age, where a damaged man without super strength can still perform righteous deeds and change the world. . . . *Mitzvah Man* will restore your faith in the miracle of simple goodness.

—**Thane Rosenbaum**, author of *The Stranger Within Sarah Stein*, *The Golems of Gotham*, and *Second Hand Smoke*

Wrestling with Angels

Clayton's new stories show a steady, assured hand, delivering an exceptional and gratifying body of work. He is a master of his material.

—*Publishers Weekly*

Kuperman's Fire

Clayton adroitly combines thriller elements with one man's particular, but res-onant, Jewish legacy. His morality tale effectively explores the courage, costs, and rewards involved in putting others first.

—*Publishers Weekly*

Radiance

Here are powerful stories of urban life in America, of life often enough among Jews who carry their exile and their wilderness within them. This is a book about victories—of the soul and of our language.

—**Frederick Busch**, winner of the American Academy of Arts and Letters Fiction Award

An easy bet for one of the year's ten best collections.

—*Kirkus Reviews*, starred review

MANY
SECONDS
INTO THE
FUTURE

Ten
stories

John J. Clayton

Texas Tech University Press

MANY
SECONDS
INTO THE
FUTURE

This book is typeset in Scala. The paper used in this book meets the minimum requirements of ANSI/NISO Z39.48-1992 (R1997). ∞

Designed by Kasey McBeath
Cover illustration by Ashley Beck

Library of Congress Cataloging-in-Publication Data
Clayton, John Jacob.
    [Short stories. Selections]
    Many Seconds Into the Future : Ten Stories / John J. Clayton.
        pages cm. — (Modern Jewish Literature and Culture)
    ISBN 978-0-89672-859-2 (paperback) — ISBN 978-0-89672-860-8
(e-book) 1. Jewish fiction. I. Title.
    PS3553.L388A6 2014
    813'.54—dc23   2013050901

14 15 16 17 18 19 20 21 22 / 9 8 7 6 5 4 3 2 1

Texas Tech University Press
Box 41037 | Lubbock, Texas 79409-1037 USA
800.832.4042 | ttup@ttu.edu | www.ttupress.org

An earlier version of "Straps and Boxes" previously appeared in *The Journal*.

An earlier version of "Getting Out in One Piece" previously appeared in *Sewanee Review*.

Earlier versions of "Many Seconds into the Future," "The Name Changer," "A Man in Thrall," "All the Children Are Isaac," and "Reading to Jacob" previously appeared in *Commentary*.

For Sharon and the children: Laura, Sasha, Aaron, and, always, Josh

CONTENTS

MANY
SECONDS
INTO THE
FUTURE

1

MANY SECONDS
INTO THE FUTURE

Almost every day now, Daniel Hirsch looks up from his desk in the Boston office where he practices law, or stands—on clear fall days—on the back deck of his house in Newton, a cup of coffee in his hand, and sends his spirit two hundred years into the future. Two hundred years, lifting above himself, seeing himself tiny down below—from that vantage point, he's on a cliff of time looking down into a valley in which, to those below, everything seems to matter intensely, while from this cliff all that turmoil in the heart is simply . . . interesting, part of a dance, a little sad, a little funny. From this cliff it's not such an important concern whether he lives until he's eighty—or only till sixty, as will in fact be the case, for this, his sixtieth year, is almost sure to be the year of his death.

Considering things this way, though alive, he's as good as dead. A hundred years from now, the difference of these few months, even a difference of a few lost years, will seem an eye blink. After all, he's not Mozart, he's not Schubert. What's a few years more or less?

At some point, he wants to believe, God will roll up the scenery and redeem us all. We'll all be our original selves at Mount Sinai hearing the thunder. As others—who knows?—will be at Mecca or Bethlehem. And God will spread a tallis of light over all of us and say, "I know how strange your lives seemed. Now that I can explain it to you, I don't need to, do I? The meaning is in your bones."

In the meantime, while this flicker of life—its meaning—is not known to him, the image of a cliff of time is deeply consoling. The air is clear up here. His head lifts. No one would know he's been dead for centuries, or that he won't be alive next year at this time.

It's just after the High Holy Days. He has not, it seems, been inscribed in the Book of Life.

His wife doesn't know. His teenage son and daughter don't know. His clients—mostly he handles estates—don't know. He's left extensive notes in each file. He's provided as much clarity and tax savings as he can. He's burned separate CDs for everyone in the family: his brother in Ohio; his sister-in-law in Denver; two old friends; his ex-wife, Jennifer; their grown son, Jonah; his teenagers, Alyssa and Jeremy; his wife, Molly. Mostly dry, practical stuff. No profound word-from-beyond-the-grave.

"Molly, please make sure that Alyssa, when she has a home of her own, gets my grandmother's samovar." And to Jeremy, "In case I leave you before the summer, the materials concerning your trip to Israel are in the bottom drawer of my desk upstairs. It's paid for. You take that trip, mister. You can say Kaddish for me over there just as well as here."

In each of the audio letters, he makes sure to say he loves wife or child or friend—or Jennifer, who was once wife.

"Jennifer, you've been a wonderful, funny, generous ex-wife to me. Isn't it a great joke that we made such terrible mates and then such good friends?" No solemn philosophizing, and nothing about God, though each member of his family knows that in a secret cave inside his chest he stokes a sense of the holy.

Is he sad? Of course he's sad. He won't be a support to Jeremy and Alyssa through college. He won't be there for their marriages, the births, please God, of their children and Jonah's children. He'd planned to travel with Molly when they were empty nesters. It's not going to happen. Is he afraid? Of course. He's been told to expect seizures and memory loss, possibly nausea, headaches, neurological incapacities. He sees his flesh rotting in the ground. He goes through bouts of panic. He's been told he's lucky—there won't be much pain. An operation might give him an additional couple of months. He's opted out. For as long as possible, he wants just to live an ordinary life. Soon he won't be able to hide symptoms; then the slope down is steep, maybe a two-month tumble. It disturbs him that at the end he won't have a lucid relationship to his family. And how will he come to God with a clear soul? If he ever needed to do teshuvah, to return, to change his life, now is the time.

A month ago he had a severe headache; he lay down for hours. "You never have headaches," Molly said. "If this lasts, I want you to see Dr. Schwab." The headache went away. A week later, just before Rosh Hashanah, as he walked across the Boston Common toward the subway at Park Street, a brilliant, sunny day, the look of things altered. It didn't happen all at once, but his visual field was breaking up: trees, faces, paths were either intensely bright, too bright to look at without squinting, or dim, deeply shadowed. Spots of nonseeing, and over everything a glow.

It didn't scare him; it made what he saw strangely beautiful. A few times at Swarthmore, he'd tried mescaline. Mescaline enriches your visual field, can turn it into a Postimpressionist canvas. The colors! Crossing the Common was a little like that. It made him stop, stare, breathe deeply.

"Classic migraine symptoms," his doctor told him over the phone. "You don't have a history of migraines? Well, come in, we'll take a look. But there's nothing to worry about."

He wasn't worried. In fact, he rather hoped it would happen again. Schwab said, "Well, you know, given the headache—and the left side of your face: you do know it's drooping?—an MRI wouldn't be overkill. Could be a tiny stroke."

Daniel was sucked into the howling, cramped coffin of the MRI. In a few hours a radiologist and an oncologist diagnosed glioblastoma multiforme, deadliest of the brain cancers.

They stared at the MRI, clamped to Dr. Schwab's light box. "So. I need to send you on to a surgeon," he said, sighing. "They'll do a biopsy. At the same time, we'll see if they can debulk some of the tumor."

"Some of."

"Right. Some. I'm afraid so, Dan. Look. Fact is, your odds are less than poor. Time is short. A few months. At best a few months.

But I'm not an oncologist, I'm not a surgeon. You go for a biopsy. I'll set up the appointment. You've got insurance."

"Let me think about it."

"Dan, no—a biopsy. Not something to think about. That's your next logical step. Please, look at this." He pointed at the MRI. "You see that spidery-looking shadow?"

"A spider? More like a tarantula," Daniel laughed. "Or some science-fiction alien. Will you look at that son of a bitch! That's in me?" Its fuzzy tentacles, as they reached out, seemed to be growing new tentacles. It wasn't *in* his brain or *on* his brain, it was etched into the pattern of his brain tissue. "I'll get back to you, Doctor. For now, let's keep this between us."

He shook hands and strode down the hallway to the main reception area. He knew that if he turned around he'd see Schwab staring after him.

After his talk with the doctor, after a little research on the Web, he knew he couldn't stop the creature from taking over. Not by surgery, not by chemo or radiation. He might win a few weeks' reprieve, but at what cost?

"It's nothing. Stress," he told Molly. "Just what you thought. I'm working too hard. I need to take time to live a normal life. An ordinary life."

"What I've been telling you."

"Absolutely. I intend to spend more time with you and Jeremy and Alyssa."

Only Harry Barnett, his firm's senior partner, and Tim Asher, his friend since law school, know the whole story. "I'm staying on. When I can't do a good job," he says, "I'll tell you. And if you see things I can't see, ways I'm screwing up, just let me know."

Harry Barnett, the old man in the firm, rests his elbows on the walnut conference table, chin on folded hands. "This is really rotten, boy. You sure you want to stay on? Don't you want to bail out? Travel somewhere? Visit friends?"

"Travel? No. What I've left unlived," Daniel says, "is ordinary life. I've lived it but scarcely knew it. That's what I want to concentrate on, and that's why I can't tell Molly or the kids. Not till I start to slide. Because as soon as I tell them, the time won't be ordinary."

Tim adds: "Doctors can be wrong, too. You look great, Dan. Maybe it's a misdiagnosis."

Daniel, a tiny headache starting up: "From your lips to God's ear."

But he can't count on this message being received. He sits cross-legged on a meditation mat in his study, and rather than focusing on his breath as he usually does, he imagines light perforating the top of his head and pouring in, shriveling the monster. After a half hour he's mellow but not optimistic.

"More time with you and the kids."

These children came to him late. Jonah, his son with Jennifer, is thirty-three, married, living in Seattle. They talk on the phone, talk eagerly of Jonah's successes—he's the youngest dean at the University of Washington—but they don't see a lot of each other. Strange. When Daniel was a very young father, living and fighting with Jennifer, he focused all his love on Jonah. Even when he was busy clerking after law school, when he'd been taken into a large Boston practice and needed to work impossibly hard, he took Jonah to Fenway, took him backpacking. Though he and Jennifer were dead to one another, he had to show that he had love to give. It's been different, easier, with Jeremy and Alyssa—he's loved them more naturally. As his career flourished, he's watched them grow up, if too often just going through the motions. It's not that sometimes he misses Alyssa's violin recitals, or doesn't always see Jeremy pitch. It's that when he does go, often only his body is there, while he's scribbling points in a notebook.

Well, except for the time of his breakup with Jennifer, he was never very expressive. She used to call him "Mr. Cool" when they were on good terms, "Mr. Chilly" when not.

"I can't stand how secretive you are," she would say. Which is funny, because now as friends they share secrets, gossip together easily.

Still, keeping this secret feels in tune with the rest of his life.

He believes it comes from his father, a man who narrowed his eyes a lot and locked his secrets behind them. They quarreled when Daniel was in high school, and then he simply cut off until he was in law school and his father near death. The big man, maybe 220 pounds, once a semipro boxer, then a middle manager for General Mills—what secrets, after all?—had shrunk sadly, flesh sagging on the big bones. He still couldn't talk to Daniel. He'd always bragged about Daniel's smarts, but was embarrassed that his son was a lousy athlete.

Daniel remembers sitting by his father's bed in the hospital. One of the last things the old man said to him was, "I never could teach you to hit a ball, could I?"

Just look at Jeremy, he thinks. There's the athlete he wanted me to be. Lean but powerful, Jeremy is a terrific pitcher, a fast wing in soccer. It must have skipped a generation. The way my grandfather's tefillin, which my dad gave me for my bar mitzvah but never used himself, skipped a generation.

Daniel puts on tefillin and prays almost every day. So why does he feel his father inhabiting his body, breathing out his heavy breath through Daniel? Maybe the connection is part of the reparations he needs to make. His teshuvah. And maybe another part is driving Jeremy and Alyssa to school in the morning instead of letting them take the bus. Actually he lets Alyssa drive, not only to give her practice but as a precaution. Suppose he has another episode like the one on the Common?

"You sure, Dad?" Alyssa asks.

"What is this? You're always so busy in the morning," Jeremy says.

"How much longer," he says, "will we be together like this? I mean, soon you guys will be out of the house. Am I right? I'm right."

"All day long you get paid to be right," Jeremy says. "Not with us. Am I right?" Jeremy, with his wild curly hair, has what Alyssa calls "attitude." One minute he's tender, climbing up on the bed between his father and mother to watch TV, the next he's uncommunicative or hostile, like Daniel himself as a teen, and scrappy with his sister. Now she wrecks his good mood.

"You have to be right, don't you? Brother dear, why don't you save it for debate club?"

"Blow it out thy bottom, dear sister," he says in a thick stage-British accent, and lifting his bottom adds a Bronx cheer.

"Dad!" Alyssa groans. "Ouch! He's so vulgar! You're really disgusting, Jeremy."

He asked for ordinary, didn't he?

Evenings now, Daniel's home in time for dinner. If Molly works late at the lab, and he makes dinner—he's always been a weekend cook—they wait for her. After all, he's less pressured at work, he's not taking on new clients.

Molly comes home ragged, sullen from battle with a colleague who seems to feel that her job is to make Molly miserable. In the past, he'd steer clear when she came home like this. Now he puts an arm around her, soothing. Each night, not just on Shabbat, he asks Alyssa to light candles, pours a full glass of wine for himself and Molly, a little for Jeremy and Alyssa. He says a blessing. They hold hands at the table. Alyssa is wearing her hair in a new way—three perfect rolls behind—and her long gold earrings catch the light of the candles. Jeremy is caught up in the ceremony, but he rolls his eyes and grins. The kids look at one another—what is all this? He pretends not to notice.

"You're our blessing," Daniel says, reaching across the table to squeeze Molly's hand. And to Molly, "You're my blessing." If not now, when?

Molly shakes her head and grins. "I don't get it. Daniel?"

He opens his hands wide. "Why not? You're all precious to me."

"You amaze me. But hey," she laughs, lifting forefinger and eyebrows, "don't stop!" Daniel has a strong baritone. He sings in a community chorus. But now he has decided to drop out—"for business reasons," he tells the director. This may be the last time I listen to the Brahms piano quartets, he thinks, closing his eyes while Rubenstein and the Guarneri play for him. And making love, slowly, as he and Molly have learned to do, he thinks, this may be the very last time.

It's not. They do it again a few days later, and again he thinks, this may be the very last time. Click, he says to himself, click, taking mind-photos.

There are dark times. He thinks about this house without him, his body without him. Suddenly, the room seems like an expressionist theater set, with faulty perspective and odd angles. He gets up from a chair and feels gnarling in his belly—as if the room were an airplane, tilting, dropping a sudden 200 feet.

At such moments, if someone were to ask him who he is, he'd have to look at his wallet. Then it's over. He remembers; the plane levels out. Molly's busy in her study, Jeremy's off doing homework upstairs, Alyssa pokes through a college guide. He finds himself, temples throbbing but not with pain, tumbled out of his chair onto the carpet, curled up, headphones askew. Light has washed through him. The Schubert is playing, still the same movement. Whatever "it" was, it's taken maybe a minute. It's starting, he thinks. Soon he'll have to tell Molly. Rousing himself, shaking his head clear, he giggles that he's so calm.

All of a sudden he yanks off the headphones and stumbles for the phone. He stands there, waiting, waiting. *Now* it rings. "Molly," he calls, "I think it's for you. It's good news."

She calls back, "Can you get that, Danny?" He picks it up, says, "Just a minute, please."

Then, "Molly?"

She takes the call, he hangs up. She shuts the door to her office. When she comes out, she's glowing. "Danny? Listen! They're offering me the directorship at the lab. Oh my God!"

He yells, "Alyssa? Jeremy? Come down here."

"It's not absolutely firm. We're talking tomorrow. I never thought—"

"Well, you deserve it."

"Danny?" She narrows her eyes at him. "You said it was good news. How did you know? Did they call before?"

"Just a guess."

"A guess? A guess?"

•••

That was the first time. You could call it déjà vu. Experiencing déjà vu, you not only know you've been here before, you have a presentiment, usually vague, as to what will happen next. Daniel Hirsch's presentiments become, in the next few days, anything but vague. He knows with exactitude. Sometimes what happens turns out not to be what he expects, but often it is. Most unnerving, he's propelled not a split second but many seconds into the future. There's a certain look to things. A vividness. Knowing in advance, he catches a sheen of light on the drapes, calls "Jeremy!" but too late— waits for the dropped cup, Jeremy's "damn!" the click of the pantry door, slush of the mop. It's more than presentiment. He feels the turmoil in Jeremy's stomach, the clenched jaw, the big breath. He goes into the kitchen to assuage—hey, no big deal—but he can feel the wall that surrounds the boy, can almost see it, makeshift and jagged. He waits, goes to the fridge for juice. After a minute the wall dissolves, turns into ordinary pride. Now it's safe for Daniel to say, "Bummer. I know how that feels. Thanks for cleaning it up."

"Sure."

And he does know—because for a moment he was within Jeremy's being. Maybe this damage is a gift from God. If so, it's a curious gift, suddenly to be thrust inside another person. He passes Molly on the stairs and feels a thick blur of love for her or from her, puts out a hand to graze her shoulder and feels her before he touches her. What does he feel? Not just love—he feels the anxiety she feels, too, though its content isn't clear. He guesses it's about being asked to be director of the lab. Or is it about him? Has she seen something? He feels family voices all around him, too blurred together for him to catch the words.

One night he lies in bed in turmoil and finally realizes that it's not his turmoil. It's from somewhere else. First he thinks it's Molly, but she's peacefully asleep. He sits in his study for a while, eyes shut, and it comes to him: his son in Seattle, it's what Jonah's feeling, something's very wrong. He makes a call.

"Dad? What are you doing up at this hour? It's one o'clock there." "I couldn't sleep. So? What's wrong?" he asks, as if Jonah had left a voicemail message. "What do you mean?"

"In your life."

"Oh. Nothing."

"Yes. There is. Something."

"Dad? What are you talking about? Everybody has something."

"Something particular, Jonah. Something's upsetting you."

"Dad? Well, yes." Now Jonah speaks in a guttural whisper, as if his hand is on the mouthpiece. "How do you know? There's a young woman. . . ." He tells him a little about her. A graduate student—he's directing her research. He thinks about her all the time.

And Elaine? Daniel asks. "How's Elaine?" He listens, he listens.

Mr. Cool or Mr. Chill, Daniel is a good listener. At work, mostly doing estate planning, he has to be. He listens underneath what clients say in order to know what really matters to them. In private life he never talks about feelings, hates it when conversations turn in that direction. But these days, feeling pulses through. He'd better get used to it, he thinks. It's likely to last as long as I do. Everything is so saturated, it's as if he can walk around inside Jonah's life. He feels the mess. He can't see the young woman, but he can enter into Jonah's relationship with Elaine. He's known Elaine for six years; he's very fond of her. What he can do is pray for them, enter their life and try to breathe peace into it.

Every day now, there are moments when he loses clarity and then his own peace dissolves. He's prided himself on his clear mind. What will he be without? He avoids talking, afraid words will spill out as babble. He's becoming thick-mouthed. The words get chewed at and can't get out. Worse, at moments he searches for himself, scanning a room the way you search for something forgotten, something lost. Yet as he walks through his daily life, nobody seems to notice.

He finds himself getting sleepy, needs to close his eyes a few minutes. Sleepy. Eyes closed, he imagines back, back, back, generation to generation, to a fiery mountain, an Israelite, his ancestor, in terror. Blare of the horn, the mountain smoking.

One evening, as he's washing up at the bathroom sink, talking to Molly about a PBS program they've watched, a program on stem cells, he feels faint, and a high-pitched buzzing fills him.

Fills . . . whom? Who is this person filled with sound? He's on a tile floor feeling warm breath on him, she's bending over him. "Daniel?" she says. "What's going on?" She? It's Molly. So he's Daniel. A moment later, he floods back into full memory. His head hurts; the light in the bathroom is horribly bright.

"Please, would you turn that down?" "Turn what down?"

"The music. No—the light, I mean." Only a little dizzy, he picks himself up, makes his way to the bed. "Sit down. This is going to be hard, Molly. Hold my hand. Hold my hand."

"You'll be all right—you must have slipped and banged your head. Breathe."

"*You* breathe. I've got to tell you something. Molly?"

She sits beside him and he takes her hand. He can't find words, then says flat out, "The thing is, I've got brain cancer. I've got a bad kind. Shh, shh, shh, please. It's called glioblastoma multiforme. It's basically . . . not operable."

"Danny?"

"I'm sorry, Molly."

"Please, no, Danny. Danny?"

"I'm so sorry. To have to leave you all. I'm sorry."

"No, no. Danny. Why didn't you tell me? What do you mean basically not operable? Did they biopsy it? How do you know it's malignant if they didn't operate and biopsy it?"

"You can see it on the MRI. I'm trying to bracket off my death. To live an ordinary life."

"Ordinary! So that's what's going on . . . Danny, the thing is you've been anything but ordinary. I've been feeling so close to you, and it's weird, here you are, I'm feeling close and you, you're keeping secrets. Honey, did you know one side of your face is drooping a little? It's getting worse. I thought it might be Bell's palsy. That's why I asked you to see Dr. Schwab. Oh my God. How long do we have?"

"A few weeks, maybe a few months." He knows he shouldn't say this, but it needs to come out. "Molly, I know you don't want to think about this, but you're so young, you're beautiful—" Twelve years younger, her curly hair uncolored, just touched with gray. A lovely, soft, placid face, not the face of an administrator. She fools them at the lab every day, dressing in masculine clothes. She'll marry. She must. He reminds himself to tell her so in a letter.

"Oh, shit. Shit."

"See? That's what I don't want to do. Bitterness just wastes our little bit of time. I want to live day to day. I won't be like this, so clear, very long. But we can have good days. I've been too busy to have days at all. I haven't been there. Know what I mean? I haven't been in my days."

"Oh, Danny, oh, Danny. Why can't they operate? Or do chemo?"

"Maybe we could scrounge a few more weeks—but what kind of life? Look, you can call Schwab. He'll try to get you to pressure me. It'll be awful, but I know you'll want to call."

"Why didn't you tell me?" she asks again but doesn't expect an answer.

All night in bed he holds her. They doze. She has spurts of weeping. At two or three they wake and fumble toward one another, comforting, stroking, until it mutates into making love. Daniel feels her weeping. They waken while Alyssa and Jeremy are getting ready for school.

"We've got to tell the kids," Molly says when they're alone. She's getting ready to drive out to the lab. "We can't pretend everything's normal and then you just . . . start failing."

"In a sense, it is normal. Right? Don't get mad, honey. It is. Every time we walk out the door we may never come back. People get hit by cars. They get heart attacks, they die. That's what people do."

"Horseshit. It's true and it's horseshit. . . ."

"Okay." He laughs. "It's horseshit. We'll tell the kids after dinner," he says. "Okay?"

But Alyssa isn't home for dinner—she's at a study session. At nine she's back, standing in the hall, book bag over her shoulder, a tall girl with almond eyes. He's amazed at the connection between them, feels what it will be like to be her when she hears.

Jeremy calls through his door—he's in the middle of something.

"Come anyway!" Molly, who's never loud, calls very loud. Jeremy comes.

They gather on cushions around the low teak coffee table. Daniel sees the administrator in his wife cranked and running. She'll handle things—handle everything. It's how she'll cope. It's good she has a way. "Your father and I have something to tell you—"

"Oh, no." Jeremy says. "No! You're not getting a divorce."

"Of course not," Daniel says. "Have you seen any signs of that?"

"Because it's like half my friends, their parents are getting a divorce and, well, they have this big family meeting first. Then, what? It better be a big deal, you're scaring me."

So he tells them. At once, Alyssa's in tears and Molly holds her. Jeremy just shakes his head; Daniel leans over to give him a hug, and Jeremy stiffens, punches him delicately in the chest. And now there's a long battle, circling back on itself, because no matter how often Daniel says an operation won't change things, chemo won't change things, the children refuse to accept it. It's as if he were choosing to die. "You've got to try," Jeremy says. "You've got to fight."

"You've been seeing too many TV movies. This is nothing you can fight. What I want is that we don't kill the time we've got left together by griping. Okay?"

They sit around the table grieving. "How will we know," Jeremy asks, "when it starts?"

Daniel says, "I'm afraid it will be pretty obvious."

"So that's why you've been driving us to school," Alyssa says. "Oh, Dad."

He can no longer drive with them to school because he's afraid he might have what Molly calls "an episode" and not find his way back. Besides, his vision is more and more blurred, and it plays tricks on him. An ordinary life? Everything feels full of his dying. The new "normal" includes everyone checking in with him from lab or school by cell phone. "Dad? You okay?" Molly takes work home so she can monitor him, though that's not the way she puts it. "I want to spend time with you." But the time is so washed in his dying that before his mind is gone, joy is gone. They're already mourning.

One morning Molly stays home to take Daniel to his office. He's been working out of the house, but Harry Barnett called last night, and the flatness of his voice told Daniel he needed to go in.

After rush hour they drive to Copley Square, park in Daniel's assigned spot in the garage, and take the elevator to the lobby. He's been feeling pretty normal this morning, but the elevator, stuffed with souls, gets to him right away. He's bombarded. He can't fend anyone off. He gives Molly a look: you hear what I hear? A chorus of pain and desire. Or just blood in his ears. He has an image of one of those Spanish St. Sebastians, pierced like a porcupine. He feels punctured, and, trickling out, begins to lose coherence. He tries to explain to Molly, who's got his hand now, but he knows he's babbling.

Upstairs, the anteroom is a visual metaphor of restrained elegance. Molly squeezes his hand and sits down to read a research paper she's brought along. "You'll be okay?" Daniel says, covering up his shame for needing her. "I'll be right back."

He walks down the central corridor, legal staff to the right, lawyers to the left. First by chance, then as they hear his name, his colleagues emerge.

"Daniel!"

"Mr. Hirsch!"

"Daniel, m'man, how you doing?"

"Hey, Daniel."

"Great seeing you."

By the pats and handshaking he's not accustomed to, it's clear that in spite of his request to Harry and Tim, everyone knows. This annoys him. He nods and waves like a retired ballplayer, weary of the sentimental accolades that prove he's through.

At the end, the corridor turns. On the left, the window side, are the bright, paneled conference rooms and, in the far corner, Harry's office.

Harry stands outside, reaches out his hand and wraps his other arm around Daniel. "Come on in, come on in." Outside the wall window is downtown Boston, the curving river. Tim stands up, Nancy Schumer stands up, Charles Harris half-lifts himself from his chair for a moment.

"Well, the sooner you go into goddamn remission," Harry says, "the happier we'll all be around here."

"Thanks."

"You believe me," Harry says, slowly, tapping his heart—an imperative, not a question. "But," he sighs, "in the meantime. . . ." The rest of his words are rushed. "Thing is, I think we need you to go squirrel-in with Charlie here—hand over your files, let him take some notes, okay?"

"Fine, if that's what you want."

"Don't get like that. We don't want it. You think we want it?"

"You know what I mean, Harry. If you want to get it over with now, sure. I have everything prepared. We both know I'm not going into remission."

Harry has tears in his eyes. "I don't want to get it over. Last thing I want, Danny."

Daniel puts a hand around Harry's neck. "It's okay, it's really okay. You're a sweet guy."

His fingertips on Harry's thick neck seem charged. Out of the corner of his eye he notices that Tim and Charles and Nancy are looking anywhere else.

"Charlie?" he says. "Let's you and me go back to my office." He's grateful that his speech is almost clear. But a visual incident seems to be starting up. The room grows too bright. The sky, the glass of other office buildings, silver sheen of the river far below, so bright, kind of beautiful, faces dim, breaking up. That's the scary part. He sits, closes his eyes. "You guys give me a minute, okay?"

When he opens his eyes, only Harry's there. "Charlie's down at your office, Danny. I hope that's okay. I let you rest a few minutes."

"Sure. Sure." He stands and stretches. "It's been good working with you, Harry." He gives him a brief hug, then holds on, and Harry pats, pats, pats.

All these years, it *has* been good—the work with these people its own reward. Unlikely ever to see Harry again. Tim will come over, a few other friends. He needs to say goodbye to the Edelsteins, who attended so many concerts and ate so many dinners with them. His old friend Paul Del Monte, who lives in Albuquerque now. And Jonah. Of course, Jonah. He can't bring himself to call Jonah.

Already, with this visit downtown, he's shed much of his life.

Now the files are gone, his profession gone, he has become free. But twice on the drive that afternoon, as he tries to talk to Molly, he's aware the words aren't coming out right. Coherent rise and fall of his voice as if . . . dissolve . . . his sentences have rhythms of English, but he knows that only some of the words are English. He hears but can't speak right. Pain in head, head thickening. As they drive, Molly gets in touch with Dr. Schwab by cell; it's to his office in Brookline she takes him.

Daniel hears her talking to the doctor. "He knows I'm not an oncologist."

Daniel can't hear Molly's answer. They leave him in the waiting room. When Schwab calls him in, it's to give him a shot of cortisone, a prescription for pain killers.

"But you've got to promise me you'll see Fitzgerald. We're talking about plain comfort, Daniel, not cure. Comfort. I'll give him a heads-up. Okay? You promise?" He doesn't want to see anyone new, but for Molly's sake he will. He makes an appointment with Fitzgerald. This afternoon, after a nap, he prints out information for Molly—his trust instruments, his file of investments, instructions to Joe Berg, their financial planner. Molly has always left these matters to Daniel. It comforts him that money is there for Jeremy's and Alyssa's tuition. He writes a covering note. He's impressed by its clarity. Easier than speech. "I suspect you won't need this house, honey. It'll be way too big once the kids are in college. Until then, you're probably better off not introducing any more changes into their lives. But it's up to you."

He means to add, "I want you to marry again." It's too hard to write that. Of course it's up to her; it's all up to her—unless he intends to stick around as a ghost. He half-feels like one already. There's awareness, then gap, then awareness: in, out. The phone rings in his head, he goes toward it, now it actually rings.

Increasingly he feels so oppressively connected that it's too difficult for him to go shopping now, painful even to walk down a crowded street. Others suffuse him. He doesn't want to talk to most friends. It's hard for him, hard for them. It's better, easier with those he loves. He writes—on laptop, hand too unsteady for a handwritten note. As he writes, he seems to enter them. Where are his boundaries? At moments, scanning, can't find himself. All defining separate self—dull pain thickening the base of the occiput and pulsing behind forehead.

A clear note to Alyssa: I suspect you'll want to stay with your mother next summer and not go to Interlaken. It's loving of you, but ask her. I believe she'd rather you went. I'd rather, too. Your music is such a gift to us. When I walk in and hear you playing, it's all been worth it!

Keeps a smile on his face, even for the young rabbi, only a year with the congregation, who pays a sick call. Visits to comfort the sick are prescribed in the Talmud; but it's this young man who needs comforting. He keeps taking off his glasses, closing his eyes and rubbing them, putting his glasses on again. Daniel wants to let him know, it's all right, it's all right. He could offer the rabbi a guess or two on immortality. Different from what we imagined. "I am not contained between my hat and boots." Once, Daniel thought this was Whitman's spiritual brag. What he's intuiting is that it's true, exactly true. He is becoming dispersed—especially into his family. He and the rabbi pray minchah, the brief afternoon service.

He has to use a hiking pole, tip covered in duct tape, to get around the house. It's necessary . . . move slow, don't stumble. The Friday after the trip downtown, after the rabbi leaves, Daniel has a peculiar feeling he himself is at the door. Taking up the pole, he goes to open.

Jonah! A suitcase beside him, having paid off the taxi, Jonah.

"You surprised, Dad? Molly called us. Which, let me add, is more than I can say for you."

"Going to call, really, really. Gladyouhere, gladyouhere, very." Daniel is embarrassed at his slurring. He holds Jonah, smells him the way he did when Jonah a little guy. Hey. My baby. His baby, the thirty-three-year-old dean of students, is showing Daniel a thin, pouting mouth—the injustice of not being confided in! He's not letting his father into his eyes. But anger, Daniel knows—he's seeing from inside his son—is a dam to protect Jonah from flood of grief. Still, Jonah's right—should have let him know.

"How's Elaine?"

"We're okay. She's pregnant, Dad."

"Oh, Jonah, Jonah—totally wonderful. Elaine!"

"It is wonderful. I was a little crazy for a while."

"I know, I know." He lacks words, and the *oh* in "know" has become hard to shape, so he pats Jonah's back and shakes head up and down ferociously.

Now, all his children there, he should have things to tell them. Profound, sticking-things for after he goes. Even Jennifer here—taken train up from New York to say goodbye, Jonah met her at Back Bay station. Jennifer wants to see Daniel now, while he, husband seven years, friend for life, still pretty coherent. But as they sit in the dining room, he has no words. He makes language, rehearses sentences. Is silent.

His consciousness opposite of profound. Ach, he's embarrassed . . . wears diapers.

He goes a little in, he goes a little out. He points to butter for his bread: hard-words-find. Jeremy has become a little too sober, not bad thing . . . for him. As if to test bond between brothers, Daniel plucks invisible string joining Jonah and Jeremy, and listens to resulting music. Teshuvah. Repentance, turning to God—what's it mean for him? Any dark evil in his life? Thinks no-no. Lot of inattention. A little bad anger. Impatience—people on one speed, he another. Well!

Used to be a sports car, now not so many cylinders. Nothing like withering brain to slow you down, better than a two-by-four to get your attention. Attention hard now. He prays, Hold Your hands me. Words bollix up. He slips out of himself, himself scattered into being of others at table. He can be Molly-Daniel or Alyssa-Daniel, but if he doesn't try hard-hard, he becomes them all together. In dull pain and constant blurred seeing, held by his little mishpachah, his family. At the same time, he begins to feel if he lets go, another reality will hold him. "Inscribed in the Book of Life." Maybe different from what we think. He has his ugly-ugly dying to get through. Organs stop receiving messages from dying brain, then organs die. Another reality? Isn't he half-held there already? God waiting? Crooking a finger?

The family at the table looks peaceful, everyone smiling, passing food, ordinary family, like family at Sinai. He knows better. Tension between Molly and Jennifer—friends, but not tonight. Jeremy wants to be anywhere else. "Hey, you looking good, ol' Dad," Jeremy says. Alyssa fingers a long gold earring to soothe herself, irritated by the obvious con. Daniel waves his hand, orchestra conductor, tries to make music from noise.

Alyssa resists. Begrudges his dying, his not fighting. At the table she says again, should think once more—operation, chemo. He sees: in ten years when she tells her husband the story, she'll say, "My dad just gave up." But now she shrugs it away. Most of the night, she's forced-smiling.

Jeremy's performing for Jonah, acting grown-up. Everyone performing. Daniel, too. His performance: everyone peaceful. Pretends not to know all upset and conflict they feel; pretends to believe surface. Let them feel they're fooling him—help them get through his dying. Like a midwife. Birth, birthing him. Molly, organization lady, she'll be okay sitting shiva. Tell stories, turn their life into show-and-tell as she lugs out books of photos for friends who make up a minyan. She'll hold Alyssa and Jeremy, hug Jonah, too, and they'll cry. Now his job is smile, smile. All at once he spots Jeremy. Knows how thick with tension Jeremy, about to break this peace with a snotty, sibling dig at Alyssa—Daniel even knows the comment, something to do with her weight. Alyssa's fantasy (silly, she's so beautiful) is that she has an extra five pounds. Her plate is piled high with salad.

Jeremy makes the dig: "Got enough lettuce leaves, Aly? Let's keep those pounds off." She gives him a look. Not sufficient. He really wants to get her. He's about to reach over to her plate and swat the lettuce leaves. Daniel knows: she'll take her plate and dump it all on his head, and then a big fight will suck up into itself unexpressed sorrow and fear at the table. End of peace. In the same instant, no plan, Daniel mimes a seizure—rolling up eyes, shaking, tumbling off chair onto floor. He lies there twitching. Everything, thank God, stops. Jeremy's action is blocked, conflict dissolves, and Daniel realizes—frustrating!—it was all exactly meant to be. Fake seizure, everybody helping, part of the déjà vu. God fooling him!

He speaks, but knows he is saying nothing. Not intelligible.

Intelligible: intellect, intelligent, tell. He tries to send out telling sentences but exactly like speaking college French has to rehearse a correct construction, remember words, and all too much effort from start of sentence to end . . . remembers "ordinary." Some joke. You think you die, first you go dim, say goodbye. But no. Another place takes you, another frame of reference, and everyone seems so far away, words far away. Silence. Silence. Somebody asking, somebody asking. Conscientious, like a good father, husband, friend, tries hard to push words out. Silence.

He stands up and with walking stick in hand like a pilgrim, trudges to bed. Already Daniel Hirsch is half-somewhere else.

Molly: Molly tugs hard at the drawer where the albums are kept. Uncollected photos spill out on the carpet of her bedroom. She catches sight of Jeremy lifted, by her and Daniel, over a whitecap that's run its course. Click. Jeremy looks two, Alyssa would have been four. Who took it? A friend? Jiggling, she pulls the drawer off its tracks; it almost lands on her feet. A glossy five-by-seven of Daniel at the helm of Paul Del Monte's boat. She picks up the load of albums, a whole life in her arms.

The rabbi has just arrived to lead an evening service. She feels looked at by a smiling Daniel. She remembers the day they went out with Paul and Sylvia—so windy, the boat, heeling way over, scared her. Hard gusts rolled the bay black; she held onto Alyssa and stayed low. She lifts up the albums to pass around. It's all supposed to be beautiful; a beautiful narrative. Already she's printed the most recent pictures and found a trove of Daniel's childhood photos to lay out on the coffee table. She hears coughing, straightening of chairs. Daniel's voice comes back. Not the words, just his voice over Alyssa's voice—Alyssa greeting latecomers. Cheating a little, pulling aside the scarf covering the mirror of her vanity, she straightens her hair, tucks in her blouse with the scrap of black fabric pinned to the collar, and hurries in as the rabbi chants the barechu, everyone standing, to begin the evening service in a house of mourning.

•••

Jonah: It's a bumpy flight. Jonah staggers to the rear of the plane, holding onto the seats, and, closing himself up in the bathroom, looks out at a layer of clouds just below. He's on his way home to Seattle after sitting shiva with Molly, Jeremy, and Alyssa for two days. An odd thing. He feels his father enter his body—not a ghost, but folded-in, skin to skin. And his breath—his breath is his father's breath. He leans his hands on the washbasin and starts to heave hot breath and tears. If there's content to this grief, it's regret that they'd seen each other so little the past few years. Well, but that's what it's like, he thinks, his career, his father's career, one side of the country, the other. Still, it grieves him. We used to be so close, he thinks. He washes his face in cold water. He remembers a line of poetry, "distance avails not, and place avails not," from Whitman's "Crossing Brooklyn Ferry." Paul Del Monte recited parts of the poem at the funeral; it was one his father loved. He takes the poem from his inside jacket pocket and unfolds it. At this moment Jonah feels his father's presence so intensely that he glances in the bathroom mirror, half expecting to see his father's face. "Hey, Dad?" he whispers. As the plane rocks, over the loud-speaker the steward calls for passengers to return to their seats because of turbulence.

Jeremy: Many years later, when Jeremy is working for the World Bank in Paris, his mother and stepfather come to pay a fall visit. It's become a tradition, these visits. Louise loves Jeremy's mother, and they have the opportunity of showing off Paris as if it were their own city. They also love it that Molly and Nathan take the children so he and Louise can spend a weekend in the country. He's worried about his mother, her shortness of breath. She walks a block and has to stop. Arms akimbo, she sucks in air. He sees that Nathan is protective, making sure they walk slowly, taking cabs in the rain.

He's a decent man, Nathan. Their romance they kept secret for a couple of years, and finally, when Molly retired, they married. Dad wouldn't mind, Jeremy thinks. He hopes his mom knows that. His dad was explicit about it that night after he collapsed at the table and Jonah and Jeremy helped him upstairs. Daniel felt better fast. Jeremy sat on the bed; they talked. "I want you . . . go to Israel, tickets, next summer. You go, you hear me?"

"Yes, Dad."

"You bring back some dirt . . . Holy Land, okay? A little. Spread on my grave, okay? Hey! I can talk like this . . . you . . . now . . . a big boy." He gestured for Jeremy to come close to him. "One more thing. Your mother. She'll marry, I think. I want that. You let her know."

During the week of sitting shiva, he mentioned it to Mom, but she waved it away and shut her eyes. Well, now she has somebody. Somebody nice, Dad. You'd really like him.

It brings him back to that night. Strange, Dad's collapse at the table, so out-of-the-blue and brief, and he recovered so fast. It comes back to Jeremy, closing his eyes, where they were sitting, what they were saying, and snap, just like that, he gets it. Why, the trickster! He knows what his father was doing. I was about to get on Alyssa's case, goof around with lettuce leaves. Dad knew I was going to act up. He faked it, faked a collapse to keep me from starting a fight and wrecking the dinner! He thinks about his sister, living in San Francisco now. They have a phone date planned for the weekend. He can't wait to tell her.

Alyssa: Alyssa is feeding her two-year-old, slapping the table and babbling blh blh blh, and Danny babbles back, mimicking but wilder. Then he starts and she copies. They echo each other while her husband Stan bolts down hot coffee and stuffs his book bag before going off to teach.

"I wish you could have met him, my dad," she says. She fingers her earring, remembers she's wearing no earring—too dangerous with a toddler who might suddenly yank—and Stan nods. "We had such a nice time talking about him over the phone yesterday, Jeremy and I." Stan is trying to make sure he's got everything, but he nods so she'll know he hears her. She tells him, forgetting she's told him before, "At the end, you know, so sad, he just gave up." She's given that version to each of several boyfriends before she was married, to her best girlfriend in college.

"You've told me that, honey. Why? Why did he give up? Was he depressed?" Stan asks, hefting the heavy book bag to his shoulder.

"Well, no, I wouldn't say so." She looks into a corner of the room, the ledge where she's put the shining samovar, as if he were standing there, her father, and she rethinks her story. "Stan? You know . . . maybe it wasn't giving up," she says. "Maybe Dad knew what was best for him."

Stan looks at the wall clock, puts down his bag, comes over to the table to kiss Danny and Alyssa. "And maybe best for all of us. At the end he couldn't talk, but he could shake his head, and you knew he was there. Often he was smiling. God, I never thought of it that way. The final month was terribly sad, of course, but maybe it would have been worse."

When Stan goes off, she returns to echoing her son and being echoed by him, dancing the same dance, two in one, feeling the boy by enacting the life that's in him.

2

GETTING OUT
IN ONE PIECE

Ben Kagan wishes he could speak to the dead. He wants to tell his Aunt Jean a few things. To thank her, simply that, for what she did for him as a child over sixty years ago.

He sees her now in mind's eye more sharply than he can see his mother. Aunt Jean wore, almost always, a modest gray silk shantung suit, Chinese pendant at the collar. He can still smell the peculiar old-spinster odor of that outfit—a bit of cologne, a bit of cleaning fluid, the stale air of her hotel closet—though when he was a child she wasn't old. Maybe forty in 1940, child of the century. Her hair—fine hair, black forever, even when she was fifty and sixty—was rolled into two stiff buns at the sides of her head. From time to time she'd pat the buns. This was hardly *hair*; it was like a wimple, part of a uniform. He realizes now that he never, never saw her hair loosened, not even at the beach. She seems to him a sort of nun—calm, restrained, severe about her own life but very kind, always trying to mollify, to sweeten the atmosphere, eliminate conflict. A Jewish nun? Well, hardly Jewish, though she'd grown up in a Yiddish-speaking household—during the war she became a Rosicrucian; it was as a Rosicrucian she'd talk to him about God.

Beside the portrait of his mother on the wall of his study he has the portrait of Aunt Jean—a woman who might have been thought beautiful—perfect oval face, high forehead, big, wide-set eyes, lovely skin—if she'd cared about what she called "worldly things."

If he's had a productive life, he owes it largely to her. But growing up—we're talking sixty, seventy years ago—he took her for granted, didn't appreciate. His mother made fun of her; he made fun of her himself For she was such a noodge, Aunt Jean. Jamming him against wall or closet mirror with forefinger, she poked in time to her lesson for that evening:

Poke. Simple B vitamins, please, Bennie. Haven't I told you what Carleton Fredericks said? And dear, I know it's hard, but you must stop eating poison. *Poke.* Sugar and white flour are nothing but poison. Would you eat arsenic if it tasted good? *Poke.* Do you live to eat or eat to live? It's too late for your father and mother. I try, but you know what they say about old dogs and new tricks. But you, you young dog, should be able to learn. I know what a smart boy you are. Oh, once in a great while is all right. *Poke.* You understand me? Are you listening to me?

Oh, he listened, but, laughing inside, he plotted how to get away.

His father was away a lot, not in the war. A lieutenant in the First World War, he was too old to fight in World War II. Leo Kagan was away in California for months at a time taking care of his old father, was sent out there on full salary by his brother, for whom Leo worked. So Ben was mostly without a father, but three women hovered over him; three women, jealous of one another, poured their love out over Ben and battled one another for his attentions: his mother; her sister, Aunt Sal (born *Sarah*); and his father's sister, Aunt Jean. He grew to expect it. There were no other children around. He had no siblings. His aunts were unmarried. He didn't have even close cousins.

"You're my whole life," his mother said. Or she'd say, "If anything happened to you, I wouldn't live a single day." At times, though Ben was alive, she made a dramatic gesture of killing herself, turning off the pilot, turning on the gas, and sticking her head in the oven. Or standing in front of the medicine cabinet deciding, hmm, which poison to swallow. "You crazy woman," his father would yell and shove her into the bedroom.

When his father was off in California, she never threatened

suicide. Of course not. She competed fiercely with Aunt Jean for Ben's attentions. She competed in culture—Aunt Jean was deeper, more thoughtful, but, though Jean worked as a magazine editor, his mother was more sophisticated. She knew the names of composers, writers, philosophers. She wept—and wanted him to pay attention to her tears—when the New York Philharmonic played on the radio. She loved the theater, subscribed to *Theater Arts*, and, whenever she could, took him to a Saturday matinee.

By the time they were in the cab on their way to the theater—both "dolled up"—she'd be using her theater voice. Still gravelly, it was the voice of a Shakespearean actress.

Ahh, she had "come down in the world. If you had only seen me a few years ago!"

When she wasn't bitter about her fall, she told him stories of the great world from which she fell. Never had she thought, riding high in the twenties, her own twenties, a "golden girl," making a lot of money, that she'd be married to "a poor schlimazel." She married what she thought would be a rich man. A "good Jewish wife," when she married she stopped work. "And look how things turned out!" But "I married him for better or for worse. For better or for worse." Never in her born days—when each spring she sailed first class to Europe, to buy and sketch for American reproduction the fall fashions—never had she thought she'd live on 84th Street instead of Central Park South. She'd hoped to invite David Sarnoff, Mayor LaGuardia, to dinner. ("Have I told you what David Sarnoff once said to me? Yes, to your mother! You don't believe me? You must think she's *très ordinaire, n'est-ce pas?*") Ashamed to invite her old, well-to-do friends, she made dinner for Aunt Sal, her sister Sal, who—"It's not her fault"—was "Sarah, a greenhorn with a Yiddish accent," and for her sister-in-law Jean, who had "all the style and charm of a Midwestern schoolmarm."

But she saved her real disgust for Ben's father. Leo Kagan sold tires and supervised the workers in the big garage Uncle Cy owned. Ben's mother was sure that he left to take care of his father because he was frightened of challenging his brother Cy. Now Ben thinks, No, no—Dad left to get away from *her.*

"Just when every Tom, Dick, and Harry is making a fortune,"

she'd say in her most elegant voice, "your father is a yes man for his brother at a schlepper's salary. Don't get me wrong, my dear, he's a good man, your father. But never in my born days. . . ." She sighed and didn't finish or need to finish.

Aunt Sal, though a successful designer of dresses, was uneducated, crude. But she was fun, foolish, less serious than Aunt Jean. Sal took him to the Russian Tea Room and treated him to pastries. She wore her curly black hair wild; she dressed loosely to cover up her plumpness, but she loved big areas of color, which accentuated it. One hand always on a hip, she romanced him or made snide remarks about Aunt Jean. Then there was her other side—her passionate class anger. As Aunt Jean poked to lecture him about vitamins, Aunt Sal drove into him the exploitation of the workers by the stinking, lousy bosses—all greedy lice.

Aunt Jean, on the other hand, didn't care about politics, never spoke about the war. How strange, when she was an editor-in-chief for a popular magazine during the war, a huge job for a woman in the 1940s.

Where did she find the time she spent with him? She took him to the park to walk her little white dog, but after the walk she didn't let Ben play; she sat him down on a park bench. When he was four, she held him by the collar and, pinning his legs with hers to keep him from moving, taught him to read. Later she taught him math the same way. As he got older she gave him problems in logic or ethics on that bench, or they read books to each other (*Black Beauty, Great Expectations*) or became excited about words—she loved roots and cognates and lugged a dictionary to the park. She pondered God with him. Or goodness. Now, in his seventies, he blesses her for her efforts, overbearing as they may have been.

Poke. "Please, you're such an intelligent boy. You must *not* criticize your mother as you did tonight at the table—no, not even when she exhibits her . . . little vanities."

Franklin Delano Roosevelt felt like his true father. Ben loved his voice over the radio. Ben and the three women gathered at the old mahogany cathedral of a radio and listened to FDR's Fireside Chats. His mother nodded, tears in her eyes. "You hear how beautifully he speaks?" His mother's sister, Aunt Sal, who hated "the lousy capitalists and their rotten stooges," choked with irritation when she saw her sister's tears. "Your Mr. Roosevelt, oh, my yes, such a lovely man. So tell me this—what has he done to save the Jews? You know what your Mr. Roosevelt cares about?—the war profits of General Motors."

Ben couldn't stand her talking about President Roosevelt that way.

Trying to mollify Aunt Sal, Aunt Jean said, "Yes, it's tragic about the Jews." *The Jews*, she said—as if they were some other people, not her kin. She spoke in sweet, musical tones. "But you'll see," she said, "God sets a limit to what even the Nazis can do."

"Oh, really?" Sal snapped. "What? The limit of the grave?"

Aunt Sal was often angry. Even during the war she couldn't hold a job. Bosses loved her designs for dresses, paid her good money, but she was so acerbic they let her go after a season and hired a kid out of Pratt or Parsons or, later, Fashion Institute of Technology, to copy her designs.

During the war, when Ben was eight, nine, ten, they all had dinner together once or twice a week. Sundays they listened to Walter Winchell and played bridge until, at nine on the dot, Ben's father would call. "How's my boy? How's my beautiful wife?"

His mother rolled her eyes. Eye rolling was big in his family.

When his father came home, Ben and his mother would meet his train at Grand Central—the Twentieth Century Limited. A long red carpet was rolled out when this train came in. The first twenty minutes was wonderful, Ben proud to be seen with his big dad. Then it got very bad. Then it got much worse. In an hour his father was full of rage. Ben, he'd yell in his big baritone, was "spoiled rotten." There was shouting behind their closed bedroom door, and next day he'd tell Ben, "It's all your goddamn fault. It weren't for you, we'd never fight." Back he went to California.

His Aunt Sal told his mother, "There are times you have to get rid of a burden."

His Aunt Jean said, "When I speak to Leo, I can tell he wants to be a good father."

"I made my bed," his mother said.

It was when his father was gone that the headaches and belly pangs began. His mother kept him home from school and gave him tea, sometimes spoonfuls of paregoric. He walked up and down their bedroom and dictated stories or poems, which his mother, cigarette dangling from her bright red lips, typed on her 1914 Underwood. She took him to Dr. Rudolph Loeb on Park Avenue. The doctor could find nothing physically wrong, but Ben liked visiting him. He was a tall man with a strong jaw, a bass voice, and gracious ways. Like FDR. After the exam, his mother went into Dr. Loeb's office for a consultation and stayed fifteen minutes, though the waiting room was full. On the bus ride home, she sighed. "I'll tell you a secret. You want to hear? The poor man," she told Ben, "likes me very much."

"Likes you? Sure."

"No. Likes me *very* much. And—can I tell you a secret?—he's dying to marry me and take you on as a son."

He waited. "Well, Mom? And?"

"I'm a good Jewish girl. A good Jewish wife and mother. I made my bed. . . ."

It's hard to remember these things that Myra Kagan said in the 1940's without judging her now, in the next century, with the eyes of a parent, a grandparent—he so much older now than she was then. His poor mother. He wants to give her advice: you should never, never use your child as a confidant, should never demean his father, at least unless you're ready to leave him. But the thing is, she criticized and she told Ben about Dr. Loeb to *avoid* leaving.

The belly pangs continued, as if he were in a wild sea or the sea were in him. The headaches grew worse. He stayed home from school a lot, lay in bed with books piled up on the covers. When his father came home hate hissed and roared behind closed doors. Sometimes he heard from one of them, "Go bang your head against the wall." Then his father was gone again.

Ben was eleven when his grandfather died and his father came home for good and went back to work for Uncle Cy. Uncle Cy gave him a small raise. This didn't satisfy Ben's mother. The fights be-hind closed doors grew louder, more bitter. There was hissing and guttural whispers. Glass was broken. The telephone was ripped from the wall. Ben, taking his cue from his mother, looked with contempt on his father. And his father knew—and waited for a chance to slam doors and shout.

At times his father tried to get close to Ben—or to the "real" boy he wished Ben would be. Or maybe he wanted to show that he could be a good dad. Once he took Ben to watch boxing at St. Nich-olas Arena on Columbus. Ben knows now that his father took him partly as a statement to his mother; he was challenging her. He wasn't going to let Ben stay a "mama's boy." They had seats close to the ring where they could hear the thud of blows and see, even feel, the sweat spray off the bodies of the fighters. The place stank of sweat. But it was the blood and the shouting that really got to the boy. His father's gruff "Hit the sonofabitch!" His father had boxed Golden Gloves as a teenager. Out of condition now, he weighed two hundred pounds, not all of it muscle, but when he'd thump fist into palm and bellow, "Use your right hand, you schmuck!" he seemed like some dangerous mythological beast. Everyone was yelling. And the blood—Ben was scared but was handling it okay until someone split open a cheek under an eye and blood sprayed out with the sweat. Drops of blood spattered his shirt!

"Christ, we'll never get the blood off," his father yelled, wip-ing with his handkerchief, cursing the cost of a shirt. At that, Ben threw up over his shirt, over his pants, over his shoes.

"Aaah, you pansy!" His father took out a handkerchief, rubbed away the vomit, and tossed the handkerchief under the seat. "A little blood is all for christsake. What did you think this was—a merry-go-round? Now I'll never hear the end of it from your mother."

Ben knew he should say, "I won't tell her, Dad. She'll think I got sick on the way here." Something like that. But no. He said, weakly, "Can we just go home?"

His father stormed up the aisle. Ben followed, smelling the vomit.

•••

There were the times he locked his bedroom door and heard, felt the vibrations of, his father's fist slamming against it, cracking fissures in the paint, dislodging the panel from the frame.

There were the times he tried to be sweet to his father, wowing him with baseball statistics.

There were times his father was sweet to him, stroking his shoulder, kissing his forehead.

There were times his father told stories of the men he trained in the First World War. He told jokes not for his mother's ears.

There were times Ben just sat over dinner at the kitchen table under a barrage of criticism—the length of his hair, the money his mother spent spoiling him with special foods—and he stared blankly at the tablecloth, while in his head, but only in his head, he cursed his father with all the dirty words he knew.

One evening, playing Chinese handball or stickball in the street, he forgot the time. When he finally came up in the elevator, the chain was on the door. "I'm gonna eat my dinner in peace," his father yelled. "You can get in the house when I finish. Next time, be home when we tell you."

The door slammed, and he could hear his mother screaming at his father. For once, Ben was very calm. The whirlwind was inside that house. He took the elevator back downstairs.

Aunt Jean, lived just around the corner at the Alden, 82nd and Central Park West. In those days it was a residential hotel. He had the desk clerk buzz her; she had him come upstairs. Even in her own apartment she wore the gray suit. Looking back, he sees that as remarkable. At the time it seemed normal. Her apartment was small but uncluttered. No—it was bare. Her tiny office she kept closed. In the main room, bedroom–living room, a polished table was covered by a cloth. There were two chairs, plain gold drapes, lamps on end tables, a daybed, and over the daybed a print of a landscape. Looking back, he wonders why there were no framed covers from *Argosy*, the magazine she edited. She offered him a slice of whole wheat bread and butter, carrots, a glass of Walker Gordon raw milk. While she fixed this meal for him, he examined the books neatly lined up in a bookcase across from the daybed, and the photos, mostly of him and of his father, on one of the end tables. He petted Butchie, her little mixed-breed dog, and Butchie licked his hands.

"I know for a fact your father loves you. He means well, dear, but unfortunately he isn't very smart," she said. He ate. "He never was. He was always a good boy, protecting his brothers and me. He always took care of his parents. He's 100% loyal. But not so smart. So what does that tell you? Ben?"

Ben shrugged.

"Tell me. Who is it who can bring peace into the house?"

"My mother?"

"Can she? Your mother is very smart, but can she soften him? What do you think?"

"No." He was caught up in Aunt Jean's rhythm. "No."

"Then who else in that house can be the smart one?" Aunt Jean looked around the room as if to seek out all the possible candidates. "Nobody but you." She was sitting beside him. She poked. "*You* have to be the smart one, don't you?" She poked. Taking Ben's hand she asked God for a blessing for all of them—for Ben, his mother, his father.

He realizes now that to poke was for Aunt Jean an act of tenderness. She couldn't hug him and give him lipstick kisses like Aunt Sal, or speak to him Yiddish nonsense words like his mother.

"Now," Aunt Jean said, in lawyerly tones (for she was a lawyer before she became an editor). "Let's make a list. What can you think of doing that will make him feel less frightened?"

"Dad? Frightened?"

"Benjamin! Don't you *know* how frightened he is? How out to sea? Your poor father. And frightened of *you*, because he's not very smart."

"He runs a bunch of salesmen, doesn't he? He does okay. You think he's stupid?"

"Especially in the heart. Now, Ben. If you don't help, what's going to happen?"

"Maybe he'll leave. Or maybe my mom will leave." He took Butchie on his lap so that he didn't have to look at his aunt.

"That's right. Wouldn't you want to be able to prevent such a thing?"

No! No, he wouldn't. It's just what he wanted. But he couldn't say that. In the rhetorical game she'd created such a wish didn't fit. Only gestures of reconciliation were acceptable. And so when Aunt Jean found a legal pad and a pencil, he began a list. "I need to apologize."

"But first, do they know where you are? Don't you need to call him and tell him?"

"I guess." He wrote this down. "And I need . . . to stay out of his way."

"Dear? You need to show him you respect him. Even when you don't. You might try . . . to admire him, the way you just did—as a salesman. Ask him about it. Ask him how he does it."

Ben nodded. The list went on. Now that he considers it, the list was shaped mostly by his aunt, solely to soothe his bear of a father. He was to get a haircut even if he didn't want one. He was to ask his father to have a catch, even if he didn't care about having a catch.

"You understand," Aunt Jean told him, "I'm his sister and I know what a fool he can be. You may be in the right, but he's not going to change. He's of the old school. So. Will you try?"

"I guess," Ben said, though he didn't think his father was of any school.

"Ben? Will you try?"

He thinks about Aunt Jean's shrewdness. Suppose he'd gone to Aunt Sal. She would have hugged him to her bosom and sympathized with him against his bully of a father. But then he, Ben, would have turned into the defeated one, the victim. Aunt Jean made him believe he was the strong one. As victor he could make allowances for his poor, foolish father.

Of course this interpretation didn't change his father's resentment. Quite the opposite. His father knew he was seen by his own son as a dummy who required handling. It didn't change the way his mother smothered Ben with love and little presents—a setup if ever there was one. She'd use money Leo made to find ways of expressing her contempt for him.

For instance, books. He remembers the time his father saw Hemingway's short stories propped up at Ben's place at the table, a gift for Ben's good grades, and asked his wife, "What's this? Another present? How much did that goddamn book cost you?"

"When you learn to read, you'll understand," she'd say—though of course his father could read; he read the newspaper every day. He grew silent and his heavy shoulders hunched up; in this posture he was dangerous. Not that he'd hit Ben. He'd bellow in his army voice and lift his ham of a fist in threat. "You—you cause all the trouble around here."

Sometimes Ben played the role of the smart one, the role Aunt Jean scripted, and wouldn't answer, and the rage would blow over. But sometimes he would smirk and say, "Oh, I'm so bad. It's all my fault." And his father would bellow, "You snotty little bastard. What kind of a boy are you?" and shove Ben, shove, shove, shove him with his big hard belly back into his bedroom.

Sometimes, when his mother wasn't home, his father walked around the house naked. Ben was disgusted by his belly but impressed by the bulk of his penis. That thick penis was itself his father's argument.

This was something his aunt didn't know about.

She came over at least twice a week, came without her dog. Aunt Jean was no cook. Alone, she ate raw eggs heated up under the hot-water tap, slices of whole wheat bread, raw vegetables. She drank carrot and celery juice made with a stainless-steel juicer, her only extravagance.

"When she comes for dinner, that's the only time she has a real meal," his father laughed.

Sometimes after dinner she corralled his father, stood him up against the wall and poked. And Leo chuckled and grinned, turning his head side to side to escape. No escape—and no defenses against his smart sister, who'd against all odds put herself through Northwestern, become a lawyer in Illinois, California, and New York, and then an editor. He'd grin and flush and chuckle. She'd whisper to him. Ben knew it must be about him, about his mother. After she'd leave, his father would say, "You and me, Ben, we've got to try to be decent. What do you say?"

And Ben would look him in the eyes and nod. "Sure." He'd shake his father's hand.

For a while there was peace in the house. But one evening, when Ben was about fifteen, his father, hunched over his checkbook, a monthly trial, yelled, "TURN OFF THAT GODDAMN FUNERAL MUSIC—I'M TRYING TO PAY MY BILLS!" Classical music, which Ben had begun listening to, was all "funeral music" to his father.

"Nice!" his mother said. "Refined, don't you think so, Ben?"

Ben hunched his head forward, puffed out his lips, and mimed a baboon scratching his chest.

This was meant not to be seen by his father, or meant to be so minimal a gesture it could be denied. But his father spotted it and bolted up from his desk, scattering papers, and the mess inflamed him still more. "You get in your room, you little fruit, or I'll beat the shit out of you."

What a snotty kid he was! He feels now, at seventy-three, more compassion for that poor, humiliated man than for the smug little Oedipal victor using classical music as a way of asserting his superiority! They were both of them humiliated—he terrified by raw male power, his father ashamed that his son was smarter, more clever, than he, and ashamed, perhaps, that his wife was staying with him mostly because of Ben.

It's odd—years later, after Ben had gone through college and married and brought a child of his own to the house, he saw that his mother and father had learned, somehow, to settle for one another, to forgive one another. She was kind to him. She seemed to love him. He was gentle and loving to her. But when Ben was ten, twelve, thirteen, fourteen, his father couldn't pass him in the hall without tightening his jaw; his mother barely spoke a word to his father not edged in sarcasm. And he, Ben, was angry at his mother for using him in their fights.

One night there was a particularly terrible fight. All these years later, Ben has no idea what started it. His father slammed a piece of steak against the wall of the kitchen. His mother said, "Say, that's an idea," and dropped a plate that splintered into shards on the kitchen floor. She was about to throw her meat at the wall, as if this were target practice, when he grabbed her. "You crazy woman!"

At that, Ben took his books and walked out. It was spring, he was about fourteen. His mother called after him but he caught the self-service elevator and walked down to Columbus. It was the time of urban renewal. A few blocks up on Columbus the tenements were coming down. Ben went to the Hayes-Bickford cafeteria on 86th and ordered a sandwich. He did his homework. At the other tables were men, gamblers, talking horses. It was a friendly place. He felt safe. One of the men, racing sheet in hand, asked him over to a table and the men asked him what he was doing there and laughed and bought him a piece of pie. He felt like a rebel. At about ten, a couple of dolled-up women came in and men at one of the tables bought them desserts. They laughed and were gone. He was getting bored doing homework. So he walked home. Quietly he turned the key in the lock, but the chain was on the door, and he had to ring.

He could see, past the chain, his naked, hairy father standing, arms folded, in the foyer.

"Dad? Open up."

"You think you're gonna drag me out of bed any old time? I've got to work for a living. I need my sleep!"

"Who asked you to put on the chain? Christ!"

From the bedroom Ben heard his mother yelling, over and over, "Let the boy in! Let the boy in!"

And of course his father would have let him in. He wanted an apology first—or at least wanted him to plead. Ben turned without a word, shrugged, went back to the elevator.

Now what? Almost eleven o'clock. Too late to call a friend and ask to stay over. He didn't want to see his Aunt Sal and get babied. There was only his Aunt Jean, a couple of blocks away.

By the time he got to the Alden and announced himself at the desk downstairs, his mother must have anticipated and called Aunt Jean. For waiting at the door, she was fully dressed in her gray suit as if it were daytime—her hair in those two metallic black buns. Butchie ran to meet him at the elevator, exploded in circles around his legs.

At fifteen Ben was still a little shorter than his aunt—not finding his real growth for another year. She stepped aside and when she'd closed the door, did something amazing—she wrapped him in her arms, held him against her breasts, or against the lapels of that stiff silk suit, and when she released him, her eyes were wet. Now, he can imagine that, self-contained though she was, she must have cried often in that little apartment. She must have cried when, after the war, a man took her place as editor of *Argosy* and she had to become a ghost writer and editor of other people's manuscripts, corporate reports, articles for scientific journals. And she must have cried out of loneliness. For she had no intimate friends. She had family, but not family that understood her. She loved a little white dog and an unappreciative teenager.

By the time Ben was in his teens, she came less often for dinner, finally explaining, "You know, dear, I can't take the pain I see in that house. I come for you—but it's hard." Sure she cried, but as a kid he couldn't imagine her crying. She seemed complete, unemotional, perfect rationality.

That night she sat beside him on the daybed. He realizes that she must have dressed, made the bed and covered it quickly, all in the time it took him to walk up to Central Park West and down the two blocks to the Alden. She put an arm over his shoulder. He remembers now as he remembered then the times she pinned him down on the park bench to teach him math. She was the only adult in his life not to let him get away with things.

Aunt Jean said, "Ben, what are you going to do about your father? He feels terrible, but he's too stubborn to admit it."

Ben said, "What a jerk he is! What a bully he is! Suppose I stay here awhile. You think, Aunt Jean? We could get a mattress, and I could put down my sleeping bag."

He knew that was no solution. The truth was, that night he didn't feel he needed a solution. He was milking the drama. While his aunt was tearful at the fighting, at his suffering, he wasn't suffering—or didn't know he was. He felt the victorious victim of his father's irrational anger. To lock his own son out of the house! To put the chain on and then yell at his son for having to ring!

Right! He was right!

Maybe, he thought, if his aunt demanded that he go home and apologize, he'd take a cab to Aunt Sal's. She'd turn his father into one of the bastard bosses she fought. He could stay in her extra room and take the subway to school until his father begged him to return. Then he, Ben, might apologize for walking out and coming home late.

Aunt Jean was busy finding a legal pad and pencil. She made a line down the center of a sheet. Putting the boxed two-volume compact edition of the Oxford English Dictionary on the coffee table in front of the daybed, she turned it into a raised desk. "Now," she said, quietly. "On the left side of the sheet I want you to make a numbered list of the ways you feel persecuted and abused. If your father could listen—and we know he can't—what are the things you'd tell him?"

"It's so late. Can't we do it tomorrow? I can sleep in your big chair. Okay, Aunt Jean?"

"*Now*, Ben. I'm very serious, Ben. I don't want to see you damaged. A life like this will damage you. There's no question. I know what I went through as a child. I know what it did to me. Do you know what your grandfather was like?"

"I don't remember him much. I know he was a rat."

"Why do you say that?"

"When I was born he gave my father a present—a belt to whip me with."

"That's right. He did. And has your father ever used it?"

"No. I'd call the police."

"Your father was beaten almost every day by your grandfather. Not your uncle Jack, not me. Jack and me he just hollered at. But your father was the oldest. If the slightest thing your father did bothered your grandfather, out came the strap. That's all he knew." She handed Ben the pencil. "Now, I want a list."

"A list? What I'd tell him if he wasn't such a moron?"

"Subjunctive: *weren't*."

"If he *weren't* such a moron?"

"He's not a moron. But that's right—a list."

So Ben leaned over the pad and began, and within a few minutes he'd covered the column and lifted the pad for Aunt Jean to read. But no. "Read it aloud," she said. And when he was through, she said, "How does that sound?"

"Well. Not *wrong*—but like a crybaby. You think? Now what?"

"Can't you guess? On the right column, write what your father feels. What he knows he feels, what he doesn't know. How he can be as terrible as that father in the left column and still believe he's a good person. And he does, you know. He wants to be good. So what would he say?"

This was much harder. By the time he finished it was after midnight. It was quiet on the street below.

"This is wonderful," Aunt Jean said. "For the most part. But when you write, 'The little bastard is snotty to me,' I wonder. I know he might say that. But what do you think he's feeling?"

"Attacked, I guess. Put-down. By everybody. Mom, me."

"So write that."

Aunt Jean phoned. She put Butchie in the bedroom, and soon his father rang the bell. He'd put on an old shirt, a white shirt with the sleeves rolled up, a shirt too worn for business. His belly protruded over his belt. This disgusted Ben. He felt ashamed knowing he'd have to cross the lobby with this man, even at one in the morning.

Now, Ben sees more, and so must have seen it then, too, but not allowed it to permeate—like a snapshot found in a box, taken up and thought about years later. He sees the sweat stain along the collar, the ink stain on one cuff. But especially the fading of the white cotton and the fraying of the collar. It's as if that shirt were a record of the wearing away of his father, who had to get up at a quarter to six, take the subway down, and open the tire outlet by seven o'clock. And then his brother, Ben's uncle, would bark orders at him, demean him and demean him. That's what the shirt says to Ben as a man that Ben the boy couldn't acknowledge.

Leo Kagan was trying to be cheerful. "Ahh, Bennie, I know you didn't mean nothing. For Christ sake, you got a worse temper on you than your old man, and I'm bad enough. I was trying to teach him a lesson," he said to Aunt Jean. "You could have waited a minute, couldn't you? Never mind, forget it. S'okay."

Butchie started barking in the next room—tentatively, muffled —but his father shot a look of hatred toward the door.

A temper? Did his father know that often at night, choking down anger, unable to answer attacks for fear of starting a huge blowup, Ben bit his pillow, thrust murder fingers into his pillow? A temper!

"Sorry," Ben said.

"And I got to get up in the morning," Leo Kagan said in a melancholy voice as if he were feeling pity for some other poor sonofabitch. "I gotta get up in the morning and put food on the table so this little putz can gobble it up."

"What? You don't want me to eat, Dad?"

"Did I say that?" He spoke only to his sister. "What the hell! Wake you out of a sound sleep. Me, could I sleep with this kid gallivanting around Columbus Avenue, middle of the night."

Taking his elbow Aunt Jean led him to the daybed and sat beside him. "Please, Leo. Try to remember what it was like for you, when we lived on the trolley line and Pop couldn't find work and we took in that Mr. Cohen as a boarder."

"Yeah, sure. And?"

"One night you took a piece of stew meat when Cohen should have had right of first refusal."

"What are you talking about? 'First refusal?' Cohen, that schmuck."

"And right in front of Cohen, Pop took his belt out of his pants, you remember?—and whipped you across the face at the table."

"Yeah, yeah, Pop had some temper, too."

"It left a red streak. You didn't cry. But later I found you downstairs under the staircase where you kept your bike. You remember that?"

"And what?"

"And I sat with you, dear, and I held you. And you wept. Remember how you wept?"

"I did, huh? No. I don't remember. What's that got to do with anything?" He shrugged and folded his arms across his chest and bowed his head, as if he were making himself small. Aunt Jean stroked his shoulder and his neck and his father let her. She took his two hands. He mumbled, "Christ, I got to get up in a few hours. It's not fair, what's he want of my life, this little—"

"Shh, shh."

Ben had been looking everywhere in the room—the heavy drapes, the weird picture of circles and stars, picture with tiny labels in Latin, that now he can guess must have been Rosicrucian symbols. But now, because his father wasn't seeing him, he could look at his father. His father was crying! Aunt Jean was rubbing his back.

When had he ever seen his father cry? Once, but he couldn't remember why. Now, something about his father's vulnerability got to him, and he found his own eyes wet. He felt terrible love for this man and wanted to go over to him but couldn't. He called out, "I'm sorry, Dad. Dad? I'm sorry."

"We didn't mean it, neither of us," his father said in a little, high tenor voice—his ordinary voice was a booming baritone; you could hear it clearly from, say, 84th to 83rd Street. Now he was making dramatic use of his own tears. But he was also the little boy under the stairs. As the beaten child he sang, "He ruined my life, he ruined my life. . . ."

"Leo, who ruined it?"

Ben figured he meant that he, Ben, had ruined his father's life, and that was just unbelievably stupid, and he hardened against him, but then his Dad said to Aunt Jean, "*You* know, *you* know," and Aunt Jean said, "Your brother? You mean Cy? You know, Leo, dear, you're a much better man than Cy. And I say this loving Cy. He's my brother, too, and I love him. But you're fortunate not to be Cy. He has to *be* Cy. He has to live as Cy."

"He ruined my life. Ask Myra."

"I don't have to ask Myra." She let go his hands. She poked him in the chest. "You listen. Your son isn't like your brother. And you don't have to be your father. You understand me, dear?"

"You think I don't know *that?*" he said to save face.

On the way home his father took his hand. That big, meaty hand of Dad's. When was the last time they'd held hands? Once it was all the time. This must have been in the spring or fall, because his father was in shirt sleeves. It couldn't have been summer because he, Ben, was carrying his school books in a satchel. His father's thick biceps were growing loose, fat. His arms emanated heat. Holding hands, they were each careful with the other.

"I don't mean to be a bad guy," his father said.

Ben nodded. "Me, too."

"What's she need a little goddamn yapping dog? It's beyond me. But don't get me wrong. You got some aunt."

Ben nodded, though it was many years before he really appreciated his Aunt Jean.

"That woman came out of a shit hole in Chicago. The same as me. I'll tell you something. She talks about me getting beat? She was knocked around by Pop worse than me. Know what I mean?"

"How? He beat her, too?"

"No, nothing like that. He just bullied, he bullied and yelled, told her to quit school—what was she doing, a stupid girl, a girl going to college when she should be bringing home the bacon like Cy and Jack and me? Or getting married. He tried to demoralize her. He told her she was worthless. Listen, there are worse things than getting smacked. But she's such a smart cookie, your Aunt Jean. She just toughened up and kept herself away from him. I don't mean she stayed out of the house. But she made herself a goddamn suit of armor. I still don't know how she got such confidence in herself. A lawyer! Well, she's so smart. But it cost. She had to become . . . who she is."

"What's wrong with who she is, Dad?"

"Nothing. Don't get me wrong. She's a little nuts, but she's a lot smarter than I'll ever be. But, well, for instance, she could never really be a wife. And she was one beautiful young doll."

There wasn't a soul on the street. Cars, black in those days, were parked almost bumper to bumper under corner streetlamps on both sides of Central Park West. They turned the corner onto 84th, passing the big corner building his mother longed to live in. Down the side street, past walk-up brownstones now refurbished and worth millions but then housing for the poor.

"Did you know she got married once?" he asked. "Yeah. Your aunt. Married for two weeks. Then she had the marriage annulled."

"Why?"

"Don't tell your mother I told you, okay?" He grinned and leaned down toward Ben. Ben felt the heat from his face, smelled the sweat and the soap. "The guy was a dentist, a mild little guy. *She said he was a sex fiend.*" He gave a sudden great guffaw and patted Ben on the back. "The fact is, Bennie, we neither of us got out of that house in one piece. As for my goddamn rich brother, he took on the world. He's making himself boss of the world. That's how he got out."

They were talking, he and Dad. Talking. It felt pretty good. It wouldn't last. Ben knew that. "If Grandpa was the way he was, why did you take care of him so long?"

"Ah, my pop? He didn't know any better. He meant well. You don't know how tough and scary things were for him. This was before Roosevelt, unemployment insurance, things like that. People starved to death. At least he didn't run off. Lots of men ran off. Lots."

Suddenly Ben knew that his father has himself thought about running off.

A yellow cab with its *vacant* light on sped by. Then a patrol car, going slow. His father put his hand on Ben's shoulder and rubbed his cheek with his big fingers. He sighed. "We better get right to sleep. A few hours, I gotta get up and open the goddamn store."

3

THE NAME CHANGER

Mel Breuer, lying in his hospital bed, listens down into himself, waiting for his aorta to burst. Not that he's impatient. It's like waiting for a train that's certain to arrive some time or other, and you'd prefer other; you wouldn't be upset if the tracks were out, the other side of the river. What river? The Styx? This is Mount Sinai Hospital on Fifth Avenue. A fancy place. It's a race, he's been told, between surgery and a rupture of the aorta. The rupture could come anytime, maybe in a month, maybe today, God forbid—his doctor and friend Meyer Lipsky has told him. Meyer stands holding a clipboard. This gives Meyer position and safety.

–I don't know what you did to your vascular system, Meyer says. The surgeons don't know what they've got to sew onto. Frankly, Mel, it's going to be dangerous to put you under the knife.

–I don't like that expression, okay, Meyer?

–We've got a great team, good people, but it will be dangerous no matter how good. Your vascular system, it's as if you were a lifelong smoker.

–I used to smoke, Mel says, as if casually.

–I didn't know that. You? You smoked? When did you stop, Mel?

–To tell the truth? Never. Not a lot, mind you, not so much, not like I used to. Maybe half a pack a day . . . *Good* days, he adds.

This is a big surprise for Meyer, for Mel has played poker with

Meyer more or less every other Thursday night for maybe twenty years, and once a year Mel goes to him to get tapped and prodded, to have his prostate poked (not without the usual uncomfortable jokes), and winds up always with a clean enough bill of health. Cholesterol a little high, blood pressure more than a little high, you need to change your diet. Mel refused to take a beta blocker. And he ate the way he ate. Then, because Meyer felt uncomfortable somehow, they did an MRI and behold.

–Cigarettes! You never told me. Meyer sounds hurt.

–It's embarrassing. *I've tried to quit, Doc,* he says in warbling voice as parody. Now he changes the subject, looks around his private room with its view of Central Park, and, changing the subject, points around the room and laughs, though to laugh hurts.

–When Eleanor, my wife Eleanor, was here in the hospital, may she rest in peace, she used to sigh, "I'm dying to live on Fifth Avenue."

–I'm glad you can laugh. We're going to have to go in there.

Mel imagines a cave full of enemy soldiers.

–I'm warning you, as your doctor, as a poker buddy, it may be risky. But without surgery, my friend, I mean, well, you understand? You're not much past seventy. I want to beat you in poker for a few more years. Tell me. Are you comfortable?

–Feeling no pain, thank God. That girder nailed into the middle of my chest, it's gone, and whatever you gave me, Meyer, it makes me teary and mellow all at once. Not bad stuff. So now, can I please have permission to use my laptop?

Outside the picture window bleak, bleak. His humor leaves him when Meyer goes. It's Central Park down below, but early March, gray and wet. For a few years now, since Eleanor suddenly went, he's been practicing dying. He retired. His nephew took over. Mel calls in to consult. Less and less he's been getting out of the house. Mel doesn't want to admit it, but everything is running a little slow, and it's harder to get through the day cheerful.

What's to be cheerful about? Only the kids. The boys are coming in tonight, Nate from Philadelphia, Sid from Los Angeles.

And Lisa, who lives in New York, will be here in an hour so they can snip at each other. With her, his oldest, he feels close enough to snip, she close enough to snip back—with the boys he's more guarded. This may be it, and he wants it to be nice. So typical. What a phony. Even dying he wants to make a heartwarming scene for them to remember.

But when Lisa comes, she cometh not alone. Maybe it's schmaltz, but he kind of wanted to look into her eyes, savor her smile, the smile she keeps for him, and hold her hand, show how brave he is about dying, remember with her the time he taught her to ride a bike or the time he slept on the couch in her and Stan's tiny apartment, at the ready to pick up the baby if he cried. It would be all right if she brought that baby, Michael, now a six-foot-something basketball player at Horace Mann. But Lisa knocks and brings into the room this afternoon something all in black. Black beard under black fedora, black gabardine coat shiny at the elbows and collar, frayed at the cuffs, black belt separating nether from higher parts. Under the black fedora, a black yarmulke. Just what the doctor ordered—a plump crow, a figure of anticipatory mourning. But clearly the guy doesn't see himself that way.

–*Baruch Ha-Shem*, may you be healed, he says.

–Dad, this is Rabbi Mandelbaum. Can you handle a visitor, Dad? You feeling okay?

–Let me guess—from Brooklyn?

The rabbi beams.

–Rabbi Mandelbaum came to our synagogue last month. You know the synagogue, you were there once, on West End Avenue? Where Michael became a bar mitzvah? Will you humor me, Papa?

–When you start calling me Papa, I take cover.

–I'm glad you're in a good mood. Rabbi Mandelbaum talked to our adult education class about miracles.

–There you go. Exactly what I need.

Now the rabbi presses Mel's hand with its stent and tape and blue veins raised like rivers on a relief map and speaks—no, chants—in the singsong used for discoursing on Talmud. Anything said in this voice carries sacred overtones.

–Mr. Breuer, every breath is a miracle, farshtaist? It's not there are miracles and then there is the ordinary that belongs to nature. Or actually, he sang it:

> *Every breath is a miracle, farshtaist?*
> *It's not there are miracles and then there is*
> *ordinary that belongs to nature.*

–This is what Rabbi Mandelbaum explained to us, Lisa says.

–Lisa, since when are you Orthodox?

–It's a Conservative congregation, but we keep an open mind. Rabbi, tell him about the name business.

–Changing your Hebrew name is not a business, Lisa.

Mel raises all ten fingers plus the tubes and wires as if fending off the evil eye.

–You want to change my name?

–I? I want? Rabbi Mandelbaum says. *You* might want. But not exactly change. This is a misconception. You add a name to your Hebrew name, he explains, a name nothing like your old name. You're Mel? So you become Chaim Mel. From Chai, Life. Fresh taste? And God willing, the Angel of Death, the Malach HaMavet, passes you by. It's not a sure thing. But I've seen it.

–Oh, please. No offense, Rabbi.

–Certainly, certainly. And then, he goes on, you have to fill the name. With a *life*.

–Papa, you've got something to lose?

–Lisa, what's with the Yiddish lilt? You? Since when did you move to Crown Heights?

–Oh, Dad.

Rabbi Mandelbaum murmurs a blessing. And the thing is, Mel laughs to himself, Lisa, Lisa, she knows she can wrap me around her little finger if she gets determined. Well? For her, why not?

He surrenders with a nod, palms up, eyes shut, lips puffed out. And so first thing next morning a rap at the door—a flock of white-coated men enters. Trolls, tall and skinny, short and round. He expects them to break into song. But all at once Mel is afraid. They must be coming to take him to the operating room—but why so many? And didn't Meyer promise to stop in? Where's Meyer?

Then he spots Mandelbaum in black, arms cradling a Torah scroll wrapped in silk, and gets it. It's a troop of Jews. In yarmulkes. These are doctors, interns, researchers, and male nurses at Mount Sinai who every day make a minyan first thing in the morning in the sanctuary downstairs. Today, in Mel's private room. And Rabbi Mandelbaum has brought the small, beautiful scroll, and in half an hour, forty minutes, they've raced through a morning service and changed names—Mel to Chaim Mel and he kisses the Torah just before Meyer and another doctor come in to relax him for surgery.

–May you live to 120 as Chaim Mel, Mandelbaum says, blessing and departing. He stops in the doorway and raises a forefinger like a lit candle. Now, he says, the question is, how are you going to fill your new name?

This means nothing to Chaim Mel.

–How, the rabbi asks, will Chaim Mel live?

Chaim Mel opens his palms and puffs out his lips.

–Who knows?

The Jews in their white coats and yarmulkes have disappeared. Rabbi Mandelbaum has disappeared. He blinks. Were they real? Did it happen? As the drug begins to take effect, he tries his new name over in his mouth, Chaim Mel, Chaim, Chaim. He laughs. It rings in his head, maybe because it sounds like chime or I'm—the mmm makes a gong of his head as he rides the gurney, the ride of his life, on the way to open his ribs and replace a length of aorta with a kind of high-tech bicycle tube.

He's home five days later by limo, Nate on one side, Sid on the other, Lisa fussing over them, opening and shutting doors. Michael comes after school.

–Hey, Grandpa Mel . . .

–Call me Grandpa Chaim.

It hurts to laugh. Gradually he heals—though, used to complaining, he's more aware of what still hurts than what's hurting less. He lives—he's been a success in the paper business—high up in a nice two-bedroom apartment on 81st near Central Park West—and so he can put his head out the window and see the Diana

Ross Playground and park beyond, can read his morning paper, a gentleman of leisure, while his nephew runs the firm that Chaim Mel, as plain Mel, sweated over for forty years. Healing, he walks the curving paths of the park, farther and farther, finally all the way across to the Metropolitan.

Only now, almost a month later, when the park is turning green, is he aware of something different inside. Something's different. Good? Bad? It's as if in the center of his chest someone's dropped something bright; there's heat and light glowing from this center. He imagines scoured arteries and the new tube carrying blood, so maybe this warm, pulsing core is what he's supposed to feel, what everyone feels who's not blocked up.

–E.T. call home, he moans, holding hand over imagined heart. Just to be on the safe side, he calls Meyer, but he can't make himself understood. It's not pain? You don't have a fever? You should be goddamned pleased.

So Chaim Mel shuts up and asks about Meyer's wife and kids, and, when they first play poker again, he doesn't talk symptoms. But, by now—two weeks after he first felt the glow—he thinks, Suppose it's the change of name. Suppose! Of course this he can't say to Meyer or to his kids. Nate and Sid would roll their eyes; Lisa would be too damned eager to agree—You see, you see?—and she'd run to call Mandelbaum, the last guy in the world he wants to see. The rabbi's got some kind of Hasidic foundation; Chaim Mel drops him a kiss-off note and sends him a check. Looking in the mirror, he thinks, funny, he looks less haggard, younger. He sucks in his tummy. It seems he has a nice, strong chest. Has that always been there? His hair, which has been on the salty side of salt and pepper for years, seems to be growing out more pepper than salt. He goes for a haircut on Columbus, and even Tommy the barber, whom he's gone to for years, notices.

–Mr. Breuer, I've got to tell you, you don't look like you've been through surgery. You look fabulous.

Chaim Mel grins at himself in walls of mirror.

–Thank you, Tommy, and call me Chaim.

He doesn't even tell himself that something funny's going on, that there's a light inside and that said light is the consequence of his change of name. Well, of course it's not. If anything, we're talking placebo. He tells himself this to feel like a rational being. He hides from himself what he wants to be true and secretly believes. When he takes the train to Philadelphia to see Nate and Marjorie and the kids, he says almost nothing. Standing in front of a Cezanne at the Barnes Foundation, he tells Nate, yes, he has a new name, kind of a joke, but he takes it half-seriously. He's had a funny experience with the new name, like there's a light inside, and Nate says, –Well, great, Dad. Whatever floats your boat. You look terrific. Marjorie was saying . . .

In early May he flies to California to spend time with his son Sid, who's finishing a law degree at UCLA. On the beach at Malibu, Chaim Mel strips down to his bathing suit.

–I can hardly see the scar, his son says. Amazing, Dad. They hire some kind of miracle surgeons at Mount Sinai?

He's grown stronger, too. He was warned not to lift heavy things. But when a shirt falls behind the washing machine, he tilts the machine, filled with wet clothes, out of the way so he can reach underneath.

–It's nothing, Chaim Mel says, shoving Sid aside and reaching for his shirt. What, sonny boy? You take me for an old fart?

Telling Sid he's going for a walk on the beach, he drives to Venice, rents Rollerblades, and skates to the Santa Monica Pier and back. This is not a new thing for him, but surprising after his operation. He takes it easy, and finishing up, he's a little winded, sure, but nothing serious.

This is the same day he shops for dinner at Whole Foods, and it's there he meets this knockout of a woman. She's in her early fifties, must have been a stunning beauty at thirty because she's still handsome as hell. And look at how she dresses—so young: a short skirt and see-through blouse.

–I'm Denise, she says. It sounds like "the niece."

–Chaim Mel, he says.

–You're Mel? You're saying "I'm Mel"?

–*Chaim* Mel. Chaim means Life.

Now she gets it, the throaty CH. –I get it. L'Chaim, she says. Right? She lights up, they laugh together. Her laugh, too, is a child's. A therapist by day, Denise is also a dancer and teacher of tango. They're both in the vitamin aisle looking at supplements.

–There, she points. That's a good one. She indicates a multi-vitamin-mineral formula. But you, you certainly don't look as if you need it.

He laughs, comfortable with her maybe because he's surely too old for her to take him seriously as a man, a sexual partner. But laughing, maybe flirting, he finds, oh my, he's getting hard. Now come on! When he was a kid, sitting on a bus, sure, he'd spot some girl and have to cover up his lap with books. Hell of a long time since he knew that kind of spontaneous burgeoning. Now he turns away from her and pretends to look at another shelf. Down, Rover. Down.

–You want to get some coffee? he asks.

–Tell the truth, she asks a couple of hours later. Is it Viagra? They're both panting. He's shut off his phone, he's in her bed, limbs wrapped in limbs. What a lovely, athletic body she has. He molds it with his fingertips. Overhead, on the slanted ceiling by the skylight, a New Age poster about love, text over fuzzy waterfall. LOVE MAKES THE WORLD GROW . . .

–Viagra-Niagara, he says. Not me. He's feeling vain like a kid, a rooster cock-a-doodle-doing, though when he was really a kid, he had little opportunity to be vain. He was almost a virgin when he married Eleanor.

–Well, you've got the stuff, Mel. You've got youth. Still, I think I've got things to teach you.

–I'm sure you have.

–Mel, she called him.

Well, so what? Does he really believe in this change of names? Yes and no. Sometimes he does. Sometimes he's sure it's the operation plus no cigarettes—more hot blood pumping through him. But to be on the safe side, he still signs his checks and his e-mail Chaim Mel. But when she says Mel, he doesn't correct her.

–Sid? he asks his son a few days later—you don't mind I spend the weekend with my lady friend Denise?

–Hey, not at all. Sid is delighted for him.

Chaim Mel likes walking, shoes off, along the beach, likes being seen with this pretty lady under the palms above the ocean on Pacific Avenue. He avoids wincing at the New Age aphorisms in bathroom and kitchen.

IT'S NEVER TOO LATE TO HAVE A HAPPY CHILDHOOD.

Why does it bother him so much? Maybe because it pretends to offer meaning to a life, but the meaning is cliché, is fake. And more and more he finds himself demanding meaning. Okay, I'm alive. Now what? He remember Mandelbaum saying he had to fill the name.

LOVE . . . LIKE SOUL . . . NEVER DIES.

But in bed, at least, there's no bullshit. Flesh to flesh, the need for meaning drops away. While he strokes her, he listens to the sad stories of her two dead marriages and sympathizes.

Aach, she doesn't mean to be false. It's not her fault. She has a limited set of categories with which to give shape to her life. Sometimes he sees her at the sink washing out a few dishes when she doesn't know he's standing there, and her face isn't pert, bright-eyed, sexy, isn't bitter with complaints against ex-husbands; her face sinks into real sorrow.

–Mel, she says. Mel, honey.

Gradually, he becomes Mel again. He looks at himself in the mirror, puffs out his chest, sucks in his belly, grins at the glow of his suntan. A Californian at this late date! He looks in his own eyes like a Clint Eastwood. Though truth be told, he isn't confident that he's a mature movie star. Denise sets her camera on delay and cuddles next to him for a picture, and he's surprised to notice on the big screen of her computer all his wrinkles.

She tells him,

–Don't worry about that. You can get rid of wrinkles. I know this cream, she says. And there's always Botox or surgery. You can turn yourself into anything. It's nothing these days.

A couple of weeks and Denise begins to tire him. He likes taking her out to a nice restaurant, likes strolling, Denise on his arm, through the L.A. County Museum of Art. He likes it when she holds a glass of champagne up to his ear and whispers.

–You hear that? It's a thousand people applauding you!

But oh, her sugary, flowing music that drips from speakers in every room! And the yoga she presses on him, and the aphorisms over the toilet, and her insistence on ridding him of flabby butt muscles by running ferociously with him up and down those paths and staircases between houses in the hills. It's also the way she whispers, Mel, Mel, like a little girl, until he forgets about being Chaim Mel and—is it a coincidence?—the glow, the glow inside, seems to be fading. This scares him.

He begins sneaking an occasional cigarette when he's by himself.

What does she see in him? Well, he's not poor. He can take her places. He knows wines and good books. He speaks a passable French and is well traveled, and she tells him he's "charming," whatever that means. But it's all on the surface. So before he and Denise can have a first fight, before Sid can get tired of his father's second youth, Chaim Mel says he's got business in New York. Anyway, he wants to see Lisa. He wants to see Lisa partly to ask her about this Mandelbaum character, get his phone number from her. Because maybe he should go talk to Mandelbaum, maybe the rabbi can tell him not just how to extend his life—which, after all, is just superstition in the first place—but how to live it.

Look at my hair, he thinks. It's not reverting to black. I'm fooling myself. It's as gray as ever. He's lost weight, but really, so what? Is that such a big deal? And suppose changing his name was actually effective. Can you make a new life out of losing a little weight?

Rabbi Mandelbaum, rotund in a black caftan, meets him not in Brooklyn but in Manhattan—on 47th Street off Fifth, in the doorway of a jewelry mall; past them, a huge room with a hundred booths.

–Thank you for meeting me, Rabbi. But what are you doing here? Among diamonds?

–Diamonds? So? What's wrong with diamonds? Come, Mandelbaum urges, taking his elbow. Chaim Mel, listen. I've got to get back inside. We can talk there.

They enter through the glass doors. The little man walks fast, Chaim Mel follows through the aisles of jewelry coruscating within glittering glass counters. But the faces, look at them—all, it seems to him, either scowling or bored. A murmur surrounds him. Voices rising from the murmur are harsh. He keeps his eye on Mandelbaum's caftan. They stop at a booth. The rabbi turns a key.

–To deactivate the alarm, he explains. So. This is how I make my living, Chaim Mel, buying and selling diamonds for my brother-in-law Joel.

–You're not a real rabbi?

–Thank God, of course I'm a rabbi. You think every rabbi takes a congregation? I lecture at synagogues on ba-olam, the world to come. I study Torah. But I have to make a living, no? So tell me, says Mandelbaum, what's life been like with your new name? You're wearing it pretty good, I see. Chaim Mel has gotten a suntan.

Chaim Mel shrugs.

–But Rabbi, who cares about a suntan? The glow inside, he says, tapping his chest—I have to say, there was a glow for a while inside, but the glow, it's fading. You understand? The question isn't a few more years. The question is, How am I supposed to live them?

–Ahh. The tubby rabbi raises a forefinger and furrows his brows. I told you. Didn't I tell you? You have to fill the name! I told you in the hospital. Ah hah. This furrowed *ah hah*—expressing what, the wisdom of the sages?—looks as phony to Chaim Mel as the aphorisms in Denise's bathroom. A fake! What does Mandelbaum know? Or maybe—suppose it's not the rabbi who's the fake. Suppose it's Chaim Mel, making himself out to be special, to assume he can find out what his life is for, can make his new name mean something. Maybe he's the cliché. Who is he, really? Plain Mel! That's who I am. Just Mel. At once he casts off his new name. It spins away from him, into a vortex, down, down.

–I'm Mel, he says to Rabbi Mandelbaum. Mel. All the rest, he thinks, is false, superstitious claptrap. Forget Chaim Mel. I might as well be Mel, I might as well go back to Denise and get something real out of the years left me.

But there are no years left him. The glow, surprising him, suffuses his body. As Mel dizzies and crumples, Rabbi Mandelbaum turns away from a case of jewels and opens his arms to catch him. The cloth belt springs loose, and the folds of the caftan, like the wings of a giant black bird or of the Angel of Death, the Malach HaMavet itself, open to take him in.

4

DREAMS OF FREEDOM

In dreams he flows over fields and over hills, leaping rock to rock—like running cross-country on a small planet, an island in space with weak gravity. His muscles have little to do but spring the free body high. He drops in slow motion to touch the ground, then leaps again. Not in waking life. Four months after wrecking his shoulder, breaking ribs, tearing muscles, and ripping up his knee—from the three seconds of December ice that spun him off a mogul and smashed him into a tree—daytimes he walks on Jupiter.

Oh, he's lucky to be alive. That he can finally lift his arm above his head feels like a blessing. As a Jew he's not very observant, though growing up he had a good Jewish education at a Hebrew day school. But after he got out of the hospital and could hobble again, he went to shul to say the Hagomeil prayer of thanksgiving for recovery from sickness or danger.

The pain has nothing at all to do with age—he's only forty-one; until the accident he competed in triathlons. Still, it feels like a *symbol* of aging; he may never compete again. He wakes from dreams of freedom to stiffness, aching. It's changing his sense of who he is: at times his face is encased in his father's face—grim, tired. He's haunted by that hard, suffering old, depressed man, sees him lugging his heavy case—he was regional sales representative for a tool company. Wearing his father, he slogs forward down the street as if a second, horizontal gravity were pulling him back.

In his father's case, fifty pounds of extra fat didn't help. It's different for Mark—he's lean, less than 14 percent body fat. He played rugby in college, in club competition. But he isn't built for rugby. Five years ago, though he knew he'd miss the club—the team effort, the drinking, the kidding after a game—he got tired of giving away twenty, thirty pounds of muscle; in every game he took too much of a beating. But he's always lived with assurance in his powerful body. To feel, since the accident, like his father—a father who had little to do with him or anyone, a shrinking, brooding father, a (let's admit it) alcoholic father—what's that about?

He tries to puzzle it out with his friend from the old days, from rugby days, Phil Casagrande. Healing, building up his body again, he spends some noon hours with Phil at a health club near their offices. Mark's part of a large, downtown-Boston law firm; Phil does imports. They make the loop of Nautilus machines, spot one another on free weights. Usually they talk easily. Today, Mark is quiet. Part of it is the pain he has to push through, trying to recover the freedom of his dreams. Part of it is the face of his father that comes to him during reps. Halfway around the circle of machines, he says to Phil, "Lately, I kind of walk around in my old man's bones."

"What? Your *father*? What are you talking about?" Phil laughs. "That poor father of yours, a sad sack and a failure? A failure and a drunk. Now—tell me: is that you? It worries me, hear you talk like that. A few lousy months, you'll see. This is a blip. You'll be a star again. Look how much stronger you are already."

"Sure. I know. Oh, I know. Absolutely." Mark goes back to doing reps on an abductor machine. What he finds it hard to explain to Phil, even to understand, is his revulsion against being a "star." His life of running and rugby, he says to himself: that was real. Meaning? Meaning there was maybe a little bravado in it, but mostly it was honest, fierce, what-it-was. He wants the freedom of his dreams, but he's ashamed—how to put this?—of what, in the daytime world, he's often made of his freedom. Pain has been a teacher to him. But it's best, he realizes, not to try to explain this sort of thing to Phil, kind as the guy is.

Phil wipes the sweat off his big face with his towel, and as he speaks he keeps his face half buried in the towel—*so he doesn't have to look at me when he says something serious.* "See . . . we're the last of the old Kings." The name of the defunct rugby club—club based in the Boston area. But Phil means more. "The old Kings are all over the country somewhere. Dave's in Chicago. Noah—where the hell is he?—in Seattle last I heard. But for me—you and me, we're it. Last remnant of me wild youth, get me? We had some damn run back then. I may buy and sell imports, I may attend birthing classes with Cathy, but I'm not ready to badmouth my youth or call it quits."

"Sure. We lived a terrific youth. We did."

"A terrific youth. Remember when we got dropped by helicopter back-country skiing in Utah? We can't do a lot of that now. We've got families. But when you talk about your father—after everything you've told me about him? You know what I think? I think it's Natalie."

"*Natalie?*"

"Tell me. Mark. Mark. Is she bringing you down?"

"Natalie? It's not Natalie."

"I think it is. Yeah." Phil jots down the number of reps on the quad machine. He looks up at the ceiling speaker and nods his head to the beat of the trashy music. "Definitely. I think it is. I definitely think so. You may not know it but she's getting to you. Snip snip. Know what I mean?"

"You got something to say to me?"

"Right. I do. Maybe it's nothing. Listen. It was pure fucking random—I happened to be meeting Cathy after work for a drink the way we do on Friday afternoons. Down near Faneuil Hall. And we spotted Natalie. You tell me. Where was she supposed to be on Friday at five thirty?"

"You're saying she was with someone? You saw her with someone?"

"A guy."

"So? A client. For Chrissakes, we're not kids sneaking around."

"We saw what we saw, Mark. I couldn't believe it. Cathy, it blew her mind. Natalie didn't see us. But listen—do you hold hands with a client?"

"They held hands?"

"Not so you'd notice. Brushed hands I guess you'd say. *Brushed.* We pretended not to notice them, and after awhile they left."

"I'll mention it when I get home tonight. Like, 'Phil thought he caught a glimpse of you last Friday,' etcetera. But lately, Natalie's been especially kind to me—all through this recovery."

"Right . . . Guy's name is Alain Mereson."

"How the hell would you know that?"

"I spotted them leaving, so I walked past the table. They swiped his credit card—he'd signed to pay the bill."

"You're something!" Laughter wells up but he tries to keep a straight face. He doesn't want to encourage Phil. Now he wipes down the last machine with his towel and tosses the towel in a bucket. Phil follows him to the locker room. Mark grew up in locker rooms. They all have the same funky smell, same forgotten balled-up socks on top of a locker. A kind of depressing home.

They strip and wrap themselves in towels, head for the showers, then the sauna, its dark odor of sweat and hot cedar. So good on the aching places.

A pot-bellied old guy sits with them on the hot wood slatted bench a couple of minutes. When he leaves, Phil sighs a big sigh and says just loud enough to be heard, "If you say so, I could just go see the guy, you know? This Mereson. I don't mean beat him up. A few choice words. Till you can take care of yourself. I mean physically. Which'll be soon."

Mark lets out a big laugh. "You *are* something. Hey. You're my buddy, aren't you?"

"Goes without saying." Phil grins and looks embarrassed. It's the embarrassment, like a child's, that makes Mark feel open-hearted toward this big galumph.

"You still got team spirit, don't you? Well, maybe we're not okay, me and Natalie. Not so okay. Me being busted-up, it's been hard on her. For awhile, you remember, I couldn't even take out the garbage, I couldn't drive, couldn't pick up the kids at school. But the problem isn't some love affair. She's probably redesigning the guy's condo."

Phil nods and nods but isn't listening. "More than *brushed*," he mumbles.

Sara and Jeremy are both in a private elementary school in Cambridge. Mark is on the board and likes to feel part of the school, part of the kids' lives, so once a week instead of having their sitter picking them up, he lines up behind the other cars on the side street by the school. He wishes they could just walk home to one of these sweet Cambridge clapboarded townhouses with bay windows upstairs and down and tiny gardens behind. Instead they live in a restored Federal-style house in Newton, a grand house Natalie has restored and redesigned partly to show clients what can be done with only a couple of hundred thousand dollars. Maybe, he thinks, when the kids are off in college they can become real city dwellers again. When they met, he and Natalie, he was studying law, she architecture, at Columbia. Their first apartment together was just off Riverside Drive. Then they moved back to Boston to take first jobs with big firms.

Brushed hands? More than brushed?

Spring is budding in Cambridge. Another week, the decorative trees will be blooming. He's in line early; from here he can see the entrance. At just past three Sara, Jeremy, surrounded by kids, explode one at a time out the entrance and squirrel into the car.

Natalie's late for dinner. Finally she calls. She'll be held up at work but make sure to save her some of that *wonderful* spaghetti, she tells them all on speaker phone. So they do, but it's not noisy at the dinner table. Mark wonders, are they picking up on his feelings or was it something in Natalie's voice? He goes back to his laptop while they watch TV in the next room. After awhile, he goes to sit between them.

It's well after eight. He's got the kids ready for bed. Natalie's just letting herself in. She drapes her new fall coat over a newel post. "How's your back?" she asks. "How's your foot?"

"Better all the time."

"I told you."

At times, she shines. She's shining tonight. She's wearing a pale peach blouse, a simple black skirt that, cut on the bias, defines her shape. A beautiful woman, he says to himself as if he were seeing her for the first time or seeing her in an ad in the *New Yorker*. A high forehead, an intelligent, forceful face, clear eyes set wide apart like the eyes of Arthur Rackham's children's book fairies— yes, a little other-worldly—with strong cheek bones, lovely skin like a child's. Natalie smiles up at him, kisses his cheek quickly, looks at him for a moment, then burrows into the mail he's piled up for her in the kitchen. Catalogue, catalogue, bill, catalogue— like a card sharp she peels the junk into the wastebasket, deals a letter, an art opening, a bill for herself, and he wonders, is it his imagination or is she working hard to avoid his eyes?

"They're in bed. Have you eaten?"

"I grabbed a bite. I'll go say good night. See you in a second."

"Well, *that'll* be a quick good-night," he calls after her as if she were miles off, his hands like a megaphone, trying to sound funny, voice and eyes following her up the stairs. He stops smiling, pours himself a sherry glass of bourbon. With the pain pills, he's not supposed to drink, but this feels like medicine. He waits for her, he waits at the kitchen table. He rehearses. *Not just brushed.*

How much does it matter to him? Suppose—suppose that in this time he's been broken, she took on a lover. Not pleasant to contemplate—but if so, he'll avoid contemplating. Lately, so many of his attitudes have turned upside down and sideways. But with pain came new ways of seeing. Last year he was one of a quartet of rising young lawyers on the cover of a Boston magazine. Natalie framed the cover and put it on the wall of his study. Now he winces whenever he passes it.

One of the psalms says God doesn't care "about the thighs of men"—meaning their swiftness and strength. Maybe it also means their ripped muscles. And maybe their investments and the kind of car they drive.

Natalie comes back to the kitchen. "Got to check my e-mail," she says.

Before she can go off again he says, "I saw my buddy Phil today."

She lifts her eyes—*God preserve me from that one*—says, "I think I saw him the other day."

"Oh. I guess you did then. Because he thinks he saw you."

"He's not my favorite among your friends. He's a big bull, a little crude for my taste. You used to play rugby together, didn't you?"

"Why are you asking? You know we did."

Now there's a gap, a silence, when everything needs to be spoken. Natalie puts away a clean load of dishes. At last he says, "I've been wanting to talk about something."

"Can this wait?" Her shoulders slump: the weight of one more burden.

"At first," he says, "after the worst of the pain was over, it was the humiliation that got me. It surprised me, the humiliation."

"You see?"

"No. No, *listen*," he says sharply. She exhales hugely and tilts her head, as if listening for an apology for his sharpness. "You don't understand," he says, more softly. "You don't know what I'm going to say."

"Sorry." They sit across from one another under the track lighting she'd had installed.

"What's so shameful about being broken? Really—nothing. I know that. So, see, there's a big gap between what I believed and how I felt. Please, sit with me. What I'm saying is how much I needed to be powerful. To be successful. You married this strong, successful guy. If I couldn't be that guy, what was I? Something's happening to me. Maybe something good. It's moving me."

Natalie pours herself a shot of bourbon and sits. "You may not know it, but you've said almost the exact same dreary thing within the past week. So don't say I'm not listening. Now *you* listen. I'm an architect. In the dear old twentieth century, there was this dumb idea that any decoration—anything not making visible the function of the structure—was false, phony. So stupid! Where *is* this authentic self? Should I walk around in a sack? I happen to love beautiful clothes, I love looking like a million dollars. I married a man proud of himself; maybe—all right—a little arrogant. So what? What's wrong with that? What is this new humility?"

He nods, and they sit, sipping whiskey. A long silence.

"I've been seeing someone," she says, as if in afterthought. "A client. Was once a client."

"I know."

"You *know*? Alain Mereson. We're not sleeping together. At the moment. But when you get through this awful time, I expect you and me to live the life we used to live."

"Mr. Powerhouse and his brilliant wife: the Edelman team."

"Exactly. This isn't a threat, Mark. I'm just letting you know things."

He grunts, retreats to his study. After awhile, she stands in the doorway, shining, smiling, holding the door jambs. "I just got off the phone. Know where we've been invited? You've heard of Alex Ashcroft? Right. That huge contributor to the Democratic Party in Massachusetts. We're invited to a party at Ashcroft's house. Incredible contacts, my dear! It's a real opportunity for both of us."

"I want you to know: that kind of party is exactly what I'm leaving behind."

"I want you to know," she said, "I'm not going to stay married to a depressive. That's not the model of adulthood I want for our children."

He's able to throw a ball again. A miracle, that's how it feels. He's out there this sunny Sunday on a playing field by the high school, trying to teach Jeremy to get more spring into his throws. At center field the boy's got good instincts—starts running for the ball as soon as he hears the click of the bat, knows where to go—none of the wobbling back and forth of a lot of kids. But he needs to put more shoulder into his throws.

"Better! Better! Enough—I don't want to get your arm sore. Or mine. Now let's get closer but throw with the same motion." Mark breaks up the throws with a few grounders. The boy's good at scooping up the ball when it takes a funny hop. Then they practice throwing hard from center field to second base. "Good. Much better." Out of nowhere a teaching from Talmud: "Jeremy? It seems I'm teaching just *you*. But think about it. The rabbis say that teaching your child is like teaching your child's child's child and so on to the end of the generations. Of course," he admits, "they meant study of the holy books and living a holy life. But why not playing ball? It's wonderful—think about it—teaching you, I'm teaching a whole infield and outfield."

Jeremy gets it, snaps the ball back. "And like your Dad taught you?"

Mark has difficulty lying, but he leaves out most of the truth: "We . . . played a little ball."

A very little. Dad wasn't home much, and when he was, he was so weighed down by the burden of his life that he didn't have the energy to play. He brooded over his burdens, adding to them. Evenings he sat in front of the TV watching sports, sipping away at a bottle of bourbon. A bottle of burden. Mark kept his eye on the bottle. Good weeks, a bottle lasted three nights; bad weeks, two nights—at times, one. It was crippling his father, and even as a teen, he was sure that crippling wasn't a by-product—*it was the point*. His mother used to say, "He means well, your father. He can't help himself, the poor fool."

Mark would say, "No, Mom. He *is* helping himself. It's like he's chopped off his own fingers. If you chop off your fingers, how can anyone blame you for not playing piano?"

"You don't know what he went through in Korea."

No, he didn't, and his father wouldn't speak of it. He'd come back broken down—that was the story. Mark expressed his revulsion by becoming a success at Maimonides, then Harvard. He applied for every scholarship he could find—$2,500 from the Boston Chamber of Commerce, $500 from Veterans of Foreign Wars, $3,000 from Hadassah. Plus a good financial aid package from Harvard. He did it on his own. His mother, the daughter of a kosher chicken farmer in New Jersey, believed in education, would have done anything to help him. But she didn't know how. And his father? All through his undergraduate work, all through law school at Columbia, Mark knew that his father, though proud of him, hated him for being successful. More: his success represented for both of them his victory over his father.

And now, as if the old man were paying him back, he haunts Mark's life. His father pools in the dark circles around Mark's eyes; he's there in the new, cautious way Mark drives.

If pain is a teacher, maybe some of the teaching he ought not to learn.

But some lessons are valid: he's learning how false he's been. His hundred-dollar shirts, dove gray suits or black pinstripe suits costing between $1,500 and $3,500, sing of his perfection. They lie; the pain doesn't lie. You're flesh; you're mortal. You're as ordinary as they come.

And music doesn't lie. Coming home from work he stays off the computer as if it were itself a virus; e-mail can wait. He listens to Schubert piano sonatas, a Dvorak trio, or, shutting the door, he sits at the piano, a Baldwin upright, and lets his fingers remember, with gaps, a Chopin etude. Natalie, passing the door of his study, sees him, light off, eyes shut, reclining—or sitting at the piano—and she says, with amusement, "Mmm. Music again, eh?"

He calls through the door, "Are your eyes rolling again? You ought to be careful. Too much eye rolling can damage your optic nerves."

Mark grew up a serious pianist and almost applied to conservatory. Recently, until the accident, he played hardly at all; the Baldwin upright he bought when they were first married has not been tuned in five years. He just had it tuned. The rush of pleasure that comes when he sits down to play that first evening on a tuned piano makes him return after dinner to play again. Sara and Jeremy, each with a hand on his shoulders, listen. End of the day, it's like coming home to a lover.

"I've always played," he reminds her. "You used to love it when I played."

"You didn't used to *look* like that," Natalie says. "So . . . omigod, smarmy."

All the time now, he makes her wince just as she makes him wince. She seems such an exaggerated version of the very person he's trying to expunge in himself that he knows there must be something wrong with his seeing. How could he have lived with her twelve years and not been bothered? Now, he's bothered. And though he tries to be soft with her, kind to her, she knows.

On the wall of her study, a framed four-page spread from *Architectural Digest* with pictures of a new 6,000-square-foot mansion she worked on for over a year. A photo of her conferring with the owners. She's come into her own, Natalie. He should celebrate her. He can't. It saddens him.

Doesn't he love her? He feels a rush of tenderness the first moment she's back from work. But then it's as if his open nerve endings are cauterized in the heat of the judgment he imposes.

Maybe the surgeon did something peculiar inside his chest; it's open to music, closed off to his wife.

Mark goes like a junkie to the piano in his study and works on the second movement of the Schubert 960. The old fingering, marked in by his last teacher, Sharon Lembeck, is enormously helpful. The penciled markings over the music make him feel as if Sharon, whose fingers have gotten swollen with arthritis and who doesn't teach anymore, were on a chair beside him.

Playing piano becomes a guilty pleasure. When she's home, sometimes he plays soft-pedal. While playing, he listens—when she's looking for a spring sweater in her sweater drawer or reaching for a pan under the stove top—listens for how much she's banging, shoving. He tunes in on the exact degree of her irritation. Then there are evenings she comes home with (as he puts it to himself) gratitude for her life—a hug for Jeremy, kisses for Sara, even a kiss on the neck for Mark.

When she does come on loving and sweet, he tightens against her.

Mark pops a couple of anti-inflammatories and ties up his running shoes. "Nice to get back to these," he tells Phil. In fact he's uneasy. And when they've parked and begun a slow three-mile jog around the reservoir, what Mark feels most strongly is the difference from his dreams. He's on a planet of oppressive gravity. He's careful where he puts his feet. For an instant, again and again, he replays the seconds of being out of control, heading tree-ward. The seconds slow, the moment of impact expands. A couple of young women run past, giggling. Phil blabs about problems he's been having with dock workers unloading containerized shipping in Boston.

Then he stops running; Mark stops running. "Well," Phil says, "the prick's not a nobody. I Googled him. He's chief medical officer for a pretty big HMO. He's French, but studied in Stanford and has been living here in Boston ever since. Part administrator, part clinician. A respected guy. A couple of years back, your Natalie designed his offices."

Mark takes off, almost sprinting. He stays ahead on the track, not wanting to speak or be seen not-speaking. Ducks float stupidly, placidly, in families. There's a lot he doesn't say.

The party is on a back street of Brookline near B.U. but remote from traffic, a little dead-end street with a median strip of grass and on both sides grand houses built over a hundred years ago. Ashcroft grew up with money, but he's made many times more than was given him and now, at fifty, he's quietly wealthy, a big contributor to liberal causes and candidates. His brother's construction firm consistently underbids for city contracts; the gossip is—though there's never been public accusation or evidence—that information on bids is passed, illegally passed. What's certain is that the family grows richer.

The Ashcrofts have hired a valet parking service for the evening. Four young attendants and a supervisor with clipboard. Mark and Natalie pull up to the house, he hands an attendant in black shirt the keys, and they walk up the stone path to the large Victorian, its cupola and tower lifting up, a businessman's castle. "You look gorgeous," he says in a whisper.

"Mmm. You noticed," she says, eyebrows arched.

He laughs, then shakes his head and sighs. "Why do you have to answer like a bitch? That's not you. Why do you have to play that role?"

"Well, isn't that the drama we play?—I'm Natalie-the-Bitch so you can be Soulful Mark."

Saying this, they're smiling, even laughing by the time they meet the Ashcrofts at the door.

Getting drinks for them at the bar, Mark leaves Natalie to her own devices and roves the grand living room made from two Victorian parlors plus a dining room. This huge room is crowded and more crowded. There must be a hundred people. He spots a few lawyers he knows from downtown, one from his firm. He stands at the fringe of a circle of men and women talking about some health insurance bill stuck in committee. A pretty woman in her thirties in a cashmere low-cut beige top stares at him. She's talking with friends a few feet away, but she wags a forefinger at Mark. "I've seen your face. On a magazine?"

"On a magazine cover. Last year—I was one among four faces."

"I don't forget faces. Especially handsome faces. Well, it's always nice to meet famous people," she says and mock-curtseys. He's meant to laugh. He smiles, the old charming self-effacing smile. "I'm Mark Edelman," he says. He can't help looking at her beautiful bare shoulders, her décolletage, her flowing red hair. She laughs a splash of a laugh and hands him her card. "My home number," she points. She returns to her friends. He catches a whiff of perfume.

Off to one side discussion of a new big-budget movie being filmed in Boston—union problems: teamsters giving them a hard time—he's about to listen in when Natalie takes his arm.

"Mark? There's someone I'd like you to meet."

Calm on the surface, he's in a quiet panic underneath.

She brings him to a heavy-set man in a single-breasted blazer. Lord! This is not what Mark would think of as Natalie's type, not at all. He's no heartthrob. He's older. His head is interesting—leonine —his face craggy; he wears his graying hair long, swept back. "This is Dr. Alain Mereson," she says. "This is my husband, Mark."

Now Mereson does something unexpected. Shaking hands, he smiles and moves surprisingly close to Mark until they're almost touching, blazer to blazer. Mark can smell his cologne and feel the heat of his breath. The gesture doesn't seem aggressive. The opposite. The funny thing is, Mark doesn't feel anger or hatred, not even competition. He has nothing against Mereson.

"I've heard about you," Mark says.

"And I about you."

They talk—make-believe talk—about the new public service corps the governor has implemented, about failures of health care in America. This, Mereson must know deeply, but the topic just begets amused ironic comments. When talk falters, Mark pats the shoulder of Mereson's blazer and, excusing himself, returns to the bar for more wine. He carries his glass high through the room, protecting it from elbows, picking up fragments of conversation. His invisibility allows him to slip away past waiters in black shirts carrying trays of hors d'oeuvres.

Mereson stands beside him at the bar.

"So tell me," Mark says, says casually, not looking at Mereson, "you have . . . feelings for Natalie?" He grins, because he sounds to himself like a father asking questions of a daughter's suitor.

Mereson shakes his head. "It's such a surprise to both of us. Why do people love one another? And why," he laughs, fingers toward his own chest, "would anyone fall in love with me? I'm not being falsely modest. Look at you, you're ten years younger than I am," Mereson says. "Who can understand love?"

Mark leaves Mereson. Down a hall he finds a small back parlor, walls paneled in cherry, French doors looking out onto a garden, a highly polished Steinway in the corner. Not much furniture: the piano, two leather-and-steel reclining chairs, a glass-topped table. It's a room meant for chamber music concerts—folding chairs against one wall. A beautiful room! He feels like a child slipping into a forbidden chamber. It's a delicious feeling. He sits at the piano and plays, as if in concert, part of the slow second movement of the Schubert 960. *Now don't schmaltz it up*, he warns himself. Schubert wrote it suffering, dying, but this music is his triumph.

On the way home this night they're awkward with each other, kind to one another. She brushes crumbs from his jacket. They laugh together about a gaudy woman at the party, a woman with a booming voice who kept saying, "I LOVE Barack, I LOVE Barack," as if she were hawking the president in the streets. But once he presses the garage door opener and they pay the sitter, they have nothing to say. He feels as if their marriage were already an unfixable broken thing. It would take enormous effort to repair it.

Next night they're both home for dinner. When Sara and Jeremy leave the table, she says, as if making small talk about a client, "You see . . . I think I'm not in love with you anymore." She moves the salt and pepper shakers to the exact center of the table. "It's very sad." She opens her hands in helplessness.

"Oh, *love*," he parodies in the most damaging way he can, as if she's said something embarrassingly gauche, as if *love* were irrelevant, stupid. "Please. Let's just promise we won't fight about the kids," he says. "If we can stay generous about the kids, I'll be very accommodating."

"I think about Alain all the time," she says, as if telling a friend. "It's as if I were sixteen."

He's sure it's true, but oh, Lord, he hates the false, dreamy way she says this. What a crumby actress! He can imagine a soundtrack in the background masking her weak technique. "You do want me to move out, don't you?" he says. "Well, of course; this is so much your house." And saying this he knows suddenly how much he *wants* to leave.

"It's *our* house—financially."

"But you designed the damn thing. Listen, we'll work it out. Financially." He leans forward across the table to take her hand. "Tell me. Do you think—really, I'm not being hostile, I just want to know—do you think with this Alain you can have the grand kind of life you want?"

She whispers, "I've been thinking about that. I've been doing a lot of thinking. I see that's not the point at all. It was only the point with *you*."

"Well, he seems to be a good man."

"So are you. So are you, Mark." She squeezes his hand and they share a look.

Sometimes he goes to get the kids; sometimes she brings them to his door. He's rented an apartment on Beacon Hill. It was impossible to bring his piano up the narrow stairs—it had to come in by block and tackle through a window. They had to remove the casement. He loves his little place. Spring: it gets dark later and later;

he walks home when it's still light. Nights, climbing the stairs and fingering his apartment keys, he feels in his bones the weight of his poor father's life. He straightens, the self-pity fades. No way he'll ever get rid of that role. But just to distinguish it from true life is healing. Inside, he pours himself a shot of bourbon and sits down at the piano.

Evenings he works on laptop in a darkening room under a strong lamp. When he folds his work away, physical pain and grief start to grow. He takes a book to bed and often finds himself in a bout of crying. But mornings he's happy; he walks past cobble-stoned Louisburg Square, down to the Common and past the Athenaeum to his office. Wednesdays, he leaves work early to pick up the kids at school and bring them to his place for the night; every other weekend, they're with him.

The kids, especially Sara, treat the little apartment like a play house, the dishes and glasses from a pretend kitchen. Sometimes Sara is sad, brooding. Sometimes Jeremy misses something from his "real" house—a soccer ball, a kind of food—and takes it out on his dad.

"How's Mom seem?" Mark asks them. Fine, they answer, fine. "Mostly," Jeremy adds.

He's practically healed. He works out with free weights; he runs along the Charles with Phil. A couple of times they watch a rugby club practice, and Phil gets out his old ball, and he and Phil toss it around. He spends a lot of time with Phil and Cathy. Phil's wife Cathy is in her eighth month, and she likes him to touch her belly to feel the kicks. He imagines, some time in the future, a second family of his own. One night she has some friends in—all couples except for Mark and a young woman, very pretty, seriously Jewish. They speak freely, and he thinks, Who knows? Who knows? Withdrawing cash at an ATM one morning he finds in his wallet the card the pretty woman had given him at the party, and he thinks about calling her. He puts his nose to the card and imagines her perfume. Then he remembers her memory of that magazine cover; he tears up the card.

He wakes without much pain. He likes the new quiet. He likes his work, negotiating for clients—it takes his mind off things. He doesn't think about how to "get ahead." So it's odd: twice in the next months competing firms call him up to talk about his "future." Then his own firm's senior partners set up a meeting with him—had they heard about the offers?—to make him a partner.

Sometimes Natalie calls to talk about the kids. There are always small decisions, sickness to worry about, celebrations to enjoy. Mark calls, too, hoping he doesn't reach Alain. He never does. Alain hasn't moved in. "How are the kids doing when they're with you?" he asks. Or, "Were there any leaks in the attic after the last rain?" Or, "When does Jeremy leave for summer camp? Do you want me to get him a new backpack?"

Talk becomes easier. They decide to hire, instead of lawyers, a mediator, friend of a friend. "I'm glad we can be so mature," Natalie says. But it's midsummer, and they still put off getting in touch with the mediator. Natalie calls when she's asked to restore a grand house on Fisher Hill in Brookline—only Mark will know what this means for her. Or she calls when she's simply blue. About to go off with Sara to Alain's summer house on Mount Desert Island, she calls to say, "It wasn't really the music, Mark. I'm sorry I was such a pill about the music. You play beautifully."

When Jeremy's back from camp, Natalie brings the kids over and Mark invites her in. Jeremy and Sara share a bedroom at Mark's. Jeremy carries his bag in one hand, Sara's in the other; Sara carries her teddy. While the kids are unpacking, Natalie says, "I'll have a glass of wine if you've got a bottle open." He opens a chilled bottle for them. They sit on cushions, between them a table made from an electrical cable spool. "The kids love your place," she says. "I see why."

The conversation feels so much like part of a play. Does he still love her? He's not moved by love. It doesn't rise up and compel him, the way, healing, he felt compelled to live a truer life.

"The kids say you're a partner now. You see?" she says. See what? That no matter how he tries to hide from success it will follow him?

Her pride in him, her assurance of his specialness irritates him. "How's your Frenchman?"

"Alain? He's fine. Sometimes we're very close."

Meaning sometimes they're not. At once he feels a jolt of eros up and down his thighs. "Who can understand love?" he asks, quoting Mereson, tongue secreted in cheek.

"You've grown so quiet lately," she says. "But I don't *mind* that," she adds.

In their bedroom the kids are squabbling. Sara has been bothering Jeremy with something, and Jeremy has taken it away from her. Mark and Natalie are silent for awhile, listening. It quiets.

"Look. I was thinking," Natalie says. "This weekend? We could let my sister take the kids. She wouldn't mind. We could spend some time together. Would you like that?"

He has to respond clearly and at once! If he pauses to think more than a couple of seconds, she will feel ashamed for asking. What if he says, *Let me get back to you.* That's how he feels. Then a door will close. But he isn't sure. He's afraid to lose what he's gained these past months. A true life is so much easier to manage alone. And absolutely nothing has been resolved. Nothing! Not a thing. Is she a woman with whom he wants to spend his life, a woman who can help him become a good man? Then he thinks about the kids, and—all right—not just the kids. He is aware of the tenderness in her face at this moment. He thinks: his *family* . . . All this before a two-second gap would make indecision apparent and embarrass them both. "I'd like that," he says.

Tonight, after Natalie leaves and the kids are asleep, he reads in bed. The luxury of sipping cognac and reading a novel in bed! But awfully soon he grows sleepy, sleepy, and can't fight it. His eyes are going to close, so he closes the book, turns off the light, and sleeps. He's running alongside some other runner, and as he passes, he sees the runner is his father. In his dream he thinks to himself, oh, he's playing Aeneas; he will carry his aged father Anchises on his back. But no, for his father eludes him, and his father has changed, is younger, stronger; and they run together, run in perfect freedom, leaping rock to rock, flowing over fields and over hills.

5

A MAN IN THRALL

My God, the meshugas. Self torture, self-torture, and then, futile, self-ridicule over the self-torture. Steve sees in mind's eye the tiny studio in the East 60s he borrowed from Jason Millet to spend one night with Deborah. It was a Friday. Deborah was taking the train to New York, she'd told Alan, to see her sister.

At dinner in the little restaurant on Third, they couldn't speak. Steven and Deborah comforted each other like sad children—or as if one of them were dying of cancer; they squeezed hands under the table. Back in the apartment, even while making love, she was crying. She clung to him as if she wanted their cells to merge, and she keened—because it seemed like the end, and tragic; or, more tragic, still more tragic, *not* the end.

"If I can't live with you I'll die. It's all I care about."

And Steve: "Our kids, our *kids*." He was seeing Joel, age nine, and Sarah, age six. He was seeing Deborah's seven-year-old daughter, Cindy. He saw their eyes, staring at him and Deborah. Somehow in his mind's eye they were all three sitting at the dining room table in Newton, hands folded on their laps. He saw Sheila's eyes all the time, accusing—before Sheila knew there was anything to accuse him of.

"We're too old for this," he said. "We're supposed to be grown-ups who *care* about other people. What is this Me-Decade bullshit that it doesn't matter whom you hurt as long as you follow your heart?"

So what happens after a love story comes to closure, love triumphant? In the aftermath, your children cry.

Your son gets into fistfights at recess. He hangs up on you. He hates you and wants you to drop dead. Your daughter refuses to spend the weekend. And your lover, Deborah, well, *her* daughter throws up. She lives with her mother and Steve—her father, Alan, has moved out—but she won't say good night, won't kiss. Deborah weeps.

The husband, Alan, goes through a period of communicating to Deborah only through his lawyer. Alan is a good man; it's a brief period. Alan Bayer happens to be Steve's dean—dean of humanities and fine arts. It was at the dean's annual holiday party that Steve met Deborah. They didn't say two words. She played Cole Porter songs on the piano. Steve sang—he knew all the lyrics. That night he dreamed the lyrics. Night and day you are the one. I get a kick out of you.

After their guests left, Deborah suggested to Alan, "Let's have them over for dinner."

As Steve crosses the campus, colleagues look at him without wanting to be caught looking, or they catch his eye and smile in collusion. Steve knows his grad students are talking. Everyone loves a love story, especially an Oedipal story, a Homeric story, in which a colleague carries off the wife of the dean, even a likable dean.

The worst pain begins when pressure eases. It's when Alan becomes reconciled and the children begin to accept the new arrangements, when Sheila remarries—marries someone with money—when three families spring from two, that's when things become hard.

Money is, of course, a piece of it. They can barely afford to live in Deborah's house in Cambridge. Steve is no dean, nor an investment banker like Sheila's new husband, and Deborah, assistant marketing manager at a publisher in Boston, makes even less than Steve. Alan, thank God, continues to pay tuition for Cindy's private school, and by cutting back on savings and living frugally, Steve and Deborah are able not to pile up debt. Few dinners out. No vacations in the Caribbean, no weekends in New York. For a while there seems something heroic, romantic, in the slight deprivation. Then it begins to rankle. Deborah swears she doesn't mind. Steve doesn't quite believe her, and when he sees her feeling down, and she seems down a lot—this is after the divorces, after they're married, when everything should be settled and sweet yet she seems sorrowful so much of the time—he wonders if she's regretting the sacrifice, if she's changed her mind about the whole thing. And he asks, and of course she swears. And then *she* wonders if he's projecting his own disillusionment and she asks, and of course he swears, and they go to bed right then as a demonstration of their commitment to one another. And in a couple of days it begins again.

And, strangely, there are times he's not all that attracted to her. Most of the time, just to touch her is enough to dissolve questions. But at times he notices a certain look in her eyes that strikes him as false, "smarmy," he says to himself, too much sweetness, fake sweetness, really a desire to placate him—and why? Of what is she guilty with him? Of what is she afraid? When he sees this, well, it turns him off. Or when things are good between them, full of humor and tenderness, still, still there are times she simply doesn't want to make love—three, four days of this—and he thinks maybe it was all crazy, this love story, a trick of his neurotic heart, and now—now he'll be caught forever inside an ordinary marriage, the kind he was in with Sheila.

Ordinary failures. She never blamed him; he never blamed her. But each felt blamed. They'd sacrificed so much, paid so much in damage to others—in guilt—that their love has to be perfect, their marriage perfect—passionate and complete. Or else, what have they done it for?

All the turmoil that first year! It cost far too much. After, they were never the same. The place of tender contact between them, contact with protective skin removed like unnecessary gloves, seemed instead . . . a raw wound; it scabbed over; it buffered passion. Less and less she played piano for him, less and less he shared the piano bench and sang. They both had jobs. Then there was her daughter, then there were his children—it took so much work to keep the kids happy.

A year later, Deborah got pregnant and the baby, Michael, healed them. He gave them something else to focus on besides their own intimacy. Their intensity—nothing has ever been calm, easy, for either—poured itself out on Michael. And for Joel, Sarah, Cindy, well, the child Michael became for them a focus for tenderness. The kids relaxed, grew closer to each other because they all fell in love with Michael. He became the peacemaker.

Now studying law in Philadelphia, Michael still plays that role in the family.

Gradually they became a marriage. There are times when things are hushed with peace. Was it a mistake? Is it so different from what might have become of his marriage to Sheila? He doesn't dare ask himself. His marriage to Deborah, perhaps ordinary, is a memorial to the mad beauty they'd shared. And the children have survived. Besides, there's Michael—it's impossible to imagine there *not* being Michael. Once, sitting with Steve over breakfast, taking his hand, out of the blue Deborah said, "It's not a bad marriage, is it?"

No! No! There's kindness, generosity, trust between them; there's love. It's a marriage. All that drama was, what?—my God—twenty-five, twenty-six, twenty-seven years ago!

Max and Ellie Fleishman come over—Max and Ellie were their first friends as a couple. Twenty-seven years ago, when families were being uprooted, Max and Ellie were young visual artists investigating new forms, and somehow this experiment in love gained the panache of experiments in painting. It gave the love a supporting myth of life as creative reinvention. Now, when they laugh together remembering the party Deborah threw for Steve's fortieth birthday, Steve brings a big leather album to the living room, and the four of them lean over the table to look at photos. Only those sympathetic to the lovers came to that party. All the celebrants tipsy, wood smoke from the fireplace, whiffs of marijuana. Tony Ames roasted him with a comic song about stealing a queen from a king.

But those pictures! How young they all were! Steve's hair, now gray as he approaches sixty-three, still black then—wild, wavy. The lines and creases that have begun to show themselves in his face weren't there yet. And Deborah, oh my!—at thirty-two she was stunningly beautiful. *No wonder I couldn't end it.*

"Look at us, just look at us," Ellie says. "So tell me—you think if we make it to our eighties and look back at pictures taken *now*, we'll think, 'How young we were'?"

Somehow, none of them can face one another. Deborah straightens and, taking the wine from the ice bucket, fills their glasses. "Well," she says, "for that matter, we still *are* young."

"Speak for yourself, dear," Ellie says a bit coolly, "you're years younger than the rest of us."

"I can't believe how gorgeous you are in those old photos," Steve tells Deborah as they get ready for bed. "Gorgeous, really gorgeous—what a babe!" He expects her to laugh—he's sure she'll love to hear this. How can she help it?—she's more than a little vain. That vanity keeps her going to the gym three times a week, running on the other days. "Gorgeous," he says again.

She hates his compliment! She sighs. After twenty-five years of marriage he can translate sighs; this one means: What's wrong with me *now*?

Can she actually be jealous of her own younger self, the beautiful woman in those snapshots? She can, she can—as if he'd gushed about a younger sister. He goes to her, wraps his arms around her and runs his fingers through her hair, no longer straight but professionally curled, no longer chestnut but, at fifty-five, dyed chestnut. *You're the same woman*, he says to her with fingers, *more beautiful to me now for having been the woman in those photos. They remind me.*

She won't buy his sugar. For she recognized it, too, looking at the pictures: her own beauty as a thirty-two-year-old, and the thing is, she both wants to wear that beauty like a faded corsage, a reminder—and hates the woman in the picture for her irrecoverable beauty.

He won't let her get depressed. He touches her with his fingers, a message massage, unbuttons her blouse, caresses her. *Your skin, I know your skin so well, the bones of your shoulders, I love them, they're not the same, but I love them.* There was a time she would have softened, opened her skin to rest against his fingers. He could have convinced her of anything, as he had convinced her, when she was thirty, to leave Alan. She stays shut down. His fingers know the difference.

Now, early spring, Heather enters the picture.

Heather Lindholm is Steve's graduate student, perhaps his best student in a seminar on modern novel. She's preparing to write a dissertation on Virginia Woolf. Just what the world needs—another dissertation on Woolf! But hers, if anyone's, might be original.

It's not, he assures himself, that he wants to sleep with her. I mean, my God, she's barely thirty years old. But he finds himself obsessing over her. He writes long, long responses to her essays. He meets her for coffee to talk over her ideas. He looks and looks into her beautiful Nordic face, watches her walk down the hall, long, lean, can't get enough of looking, has to keep himself from looking. Her blonde hair, days she doesn't pin it up, falls to the middle of her back. So what? Why become obsessed with the length of someone's hair or her soft skin? Why does he want to lay his cheek against that skin? He has the crazy idea it's that picture of Deborah that's done it—though Deborah is dark, Heather blonde. But Heather is thirty, as was Deborah when they met.

This goes on for weeks. Always he's been a little in love with one of his students, sometimes more than one. His tenderness is safe enough—the students are like his children. He wants to help them. This time his tenderness is not so safe. For Heather responds to him deeply. She asks for his cell number and calls to talk about Woolf's letters. Then about the young man she's been seeing. Then about her alcoholic father, though he's not part of her life now. Then about her depressive moods. One night on the phone she cries—he presses the cell phone to his ear so Deborah in the next room won't hear. It seems mysterious to him, her clear, fresh blonde looks torqued against her sadness. He wants to succor her. *My God, she's half my age—less.*

One morning as he's driving to campus he takes her call. She's decided to break up with her boyfriend. She can't imagine living a rich, deep life with that man. It's good she had the courage, but she's, well, very sad. And she's got problems, she sighs, changing the music of this conversation, trying to place Clive Bell in Virginia's life. After all, isn't her sister Vanessa her deepest love? Was Virginia's flirtation with Clive a surrogate for her relation to her sister? "There's a letter I want to show you if you have a few minutes," she says.

He folds the cell away and turns off Memorial Drive toward the Boston side of the Charles. He's afraid that if he visits her this morning, they'll end up in bed. It's as if the car has taken control. Dear God, please help me. But the old Camry drives him past B.U. into the back streets of Brookline. Though never before has he visited, he knows where she lives. For out of curiosity he's driven past her apartment building near a little park. "We're grown-ups," he says aloud. Still, it's best if we go to Coolidge Corner for coffee.

Heather lives on the third floor. No elevator. He remembers from when he was a grad student climbing stairs like these to visit young women in student apartments. Long, long ago.

But it's not a student apartment. The furniture, unmatched but fine and old, substantial, suggests to him that she must have family money. It's clean, bright, with a big bay window. She's wearing jeans and a silk blouse, peach; her breasts, small and high, catch the sunlight. Her hair, usually pinned, is loose, blonde, full. He doesn't want to leave the decent life he's made, but his body is flush with erotic warmth. If he says to her, *I think we'd better go have coffee somewhere*, the implication that he's keeping himself from his desire will be obvious, and then, of course, the implication that she'd want to go to bed with him, that she's created this meeting to go to bed with him, that their desires are the same. And then, the transgressive quality of such desire is so evident to him and must be to her—as if he's her father, her uncle.

She makes tea. He goes to the bay window and looks out over the park. It's April, still chilly, the trees leafless, but little kids are playing on the climbing structure. They sit together, Steve and

Heather, on her raggedy sofa, and, folding her long legs under her, she reads the letter from Virginia to her brother-in-law Clive: "Why do you torment me with half-uttered and ambiguous sentences?" Heather has a breathy, husky voice, and sitting close together this way, it's as if she's saying this to Steve. Well, of *course* she's saying it to Steve. He breathes in her perfume. They're in a charged space. It's as if right now, at this moment, they're already making love. What stops him from touching her, from questioning her with his eyes, isn't that he's shy, isn't that it's hard to change their relationship. It would be easier to do so, for the tension between them is so awful. He's on a cliff in a dream, and all he has to do is let go and he'll fly.

The very edge. He pulls back, stretches, takes a breath. "There's no evidence they ever slept together. But I'm sure you're right, Heather—her relationship to Clive was really part of the dynamics of Virginia and her sister." They're silent. "Well. I've got to go," he says. "I've got a meeting on campus."

He sits in his car shaking. Breathing. Crying. He accuses himself of being a fool. He accuses himself of being a coward, not living the truth in his life. He accuses himself of being a fool.

He sees Heather only in class. She calls, they talk about her dissertation.

She calls again, a couple of weeks later, a little drunk. He's sure she's been drinking. It's eight at night. Heather says, "I really need to see you. Steve? Can you come over?"

Of course he can't come over. Just to speak to her with Deborah in the house frightens him.

"I'm afraid you have to come over. You don't know how upset you've made me."

"Heather."

"It's not going to go away, Steve. It's not going to end like this."

"What's not going to end? Heather? What?"

"Oh, sure. I was afraid you'd play it that way. Tell me. Does Deborah know about us?"

"I forgot," he says to Deborah, "I've got a committee meeting tonight." Deborah, her hair pinned up to keep it out of the way, is working on a spreadsheet; she nods, she waves.

They meet at a bar on Commonwealth. A young-person's bar, a singles bar, it's crowded on weekends, but this is a Tuesday night. He's by far the oldest person there. The place is decorated with hanging ships' lamps; fish nets with tiny lights enmeshed give the illusion of a dropped ceiling; posters from *To Have and Have Not*, from *Only Angels Have Wings*, posters of 1930s movie stars fill the walls. He orders beers for them. "You've been upset lately. You're so smart, Heather—I hate to see you get this way."

"I know." She puts her hand over his, comforting. "I know you do. It doesn't have to go badly. You know I don't want to break up your marriage."

"God forbid." Carefully he withdraws his hand. "Of course you're right, it's true, there's a lot between us." But, he says, he's in a good marriage, and besides, well, he's not a young man. Doesn't she see how crazy—to take it further? "Let's leave it as a mentor who feels tenderness for his student and a student who cares about her mentor. Isn't that enough?"

"But. . . ." she looks straight into his eyes and shakes her head, "that's not the full truth."

"Oh," he says, hunkering down over the table and half-whispering, "the *truth*. The truth is, I am beginning to feel harassed right now."

In her sweet, breathy voice, as if she were speaking of love, she says, says slowly, "Steve, Steve, we both know that isn't how the university will define *harassment* in this situation."

He drives her back the three blocks to her apartment. She leans across the emergency brake to rest on his shoulder. Her blonde hair has come out of its pins; it spills over his shirt. At the light he turns to her, cups her face in his hand, and kisses her. Her skin is like a child's. "I can't stay long," he says.

It's the kind of lovemaking he hasn't known for years. It's better, because, older, he has restraint—can last a long, long time. When she comes, she scratches him just a little. She comes and builds and comes again. And now he lets himself go, and danger is stirred into the brew of sex, of youth and age. He howls. She hushes him. She rubs the hair at the back of his neck.

He examines himself naked in the full-length mirror in his bathroom. From Deborah, downstairs, he hears a passage from a Schubert sonata, an *opus posthumous*, over and over till it becomes smooth. Using the hand mirror he check on the scratches Heather made; they hardly show. He's in good shape for a man in his sixties. The slightest fat on belly or hips. The muscles of chest and arms, never powerful, aren't slack. Steve's a runner, he still takes training in martial arts; he eats carefully. Looking at himself the way he never looks, he sees the lines from above his nostrils to the sides of his mouth—but really they're smile-creases. He has no wattle under his chin.

. . . Disgusting vanity! All at once his life, a delicate architecture, a fabrication not triangulated, shaken by wind, tumbles in a heap. His life is destroyed. No, no!—*he* has destroyed his life.

Heather learns that she can reach him on his way to school. Steve learns that she's almost always at home evenings, except when she goes with a friend to a concert. Wouldn't it be wonderful to be able to go to a concert together? she sighs into her phone one morning as he's negotiating traffic. Staring at the cell, thinking how to reply, he lets the Camry slide to the right, where it's almost sideswiped.

"This can't last," she whispers to him the second time he spends an afternoon with her. She rubs his cheek as if he were her baby, her puppy. It embarrasses him, how much he loves it. "I don't want to hurt you, Steve. I've taken so much from you. Not just as my mentor, understand?"

"Sure. My sanity," he laughs. "That's all." He lies nose to nose with her in her queen-sized bed, her beauty in his hands. She wraps him in her long legs. Her thighs are so strong, her belly so lean. She glows. Her youth almost makes him angry. He doesn't tell her, *This beauty is yours only a little while.* His eyes close. Oh, he's fallen off the cliff, they're flying together on one set of wings. He imagines breaking it off, imagines her calling the ombudsman, calling Deborah. That fear, part of how he got here, is now diminished. Less wary, he feels more intensely both his own crazy passion and his shame. For even if he breaks it off and nothing catastrophic happens, still, he's the person who has done this. He'll always be that person. And the truth is, he doesn't want to break it off. He wants and doesn't want to go back to being the ordinary husband he had been: scholar and teacher slipping out of date toward retirement and old age.

"You should have known me when I was young," he says. It's meant to sound funny. Heather doesn't laugh on cue or tell him how young he is. She says, examining him, "You're young enough for me. You're still a handsome man. You *are*. You're . . . craggy," she laughs. "And I love that broad forehead of yours covering all those brains." She taps his temples.

"That's called a receding hairline."

"Steve, think about it. If I want someone young, don't you think I can find him?"

Steve realizes how little he knows about Heather. He knows she took her BA at Berkeley. He knows her parents have split up; her father is, "at last report," a businessman in Seattle; her mother teaches sociology at UCLA. It's her mother whose family is wealthy.

Her parents are both younger than he.

He learns these disjointed facts about her. But he doesn't know her. He's alien to her age, her culture, her life. Sometimes, in bed in an afternoon, she begins to cry for no reason. He soothes but doesn't understand. Her bathroom, with its makeup pots and tiny brushes, seems foreign; her music—contemporary jazz—deeply foreign. Some nights she goes with friends to dance to what she calls "techno." "Techno? Play some for me." She does; as he fears, he hears it as abrasive noise.

When she tells him stories of her father, she gets a music in her voice, a music of pain. He'd drink himself night after night into unconsciousness. Her mother finally "dismissed" him; Heather hardly sees him. She grew up in San Diego. She's a surfer—*You didn't know that, did you?*—No, nor did he know that she used to be a competitive skier, good enough to be given equipment and money by a corporation. Above her bed is a poster of a woman skier lifting up from a mogul. "Is that you?" She nods, he laughs. It was only in her junior year at Berkeley, she tells him, that she understood how much she loved literature.

"You're very, very good at it."

"You're an inspiration to me. No, I mean it, Steve."

He feels like nobody's inspiration. Guilt and shame coat his experience so thoroughly that it surprises him Deborah can't see. And yet he's not *just* ashamed, not just afraid of being found out. He's enthralled, in thrall, and also—admit it!—glorying in his own revival. That she, far and away the most beautiful woman among the grad students, has chosen him! Walking into his graduate seminar and seeing her sitting by the window, where she's always sat, chin cupped in her palm, he's both leading a class and speaking privately to Heather. His secret energizes him. He's aware of her all the time. Never a stud, a wild lover, now he walks through the world in an erotic glow.

He begins to bring her gifts—a bonsai in a ceramic dish, a first edition of Woolf's *Between the Acts*, insights. They spend a late afternoon in her bed, reading a letter to Roger Fry, a paragraph of *To the Lighthouse*. He's brought her a bottle of bourbon; he pours a shot for her, a shot for him. Well, it's five o'clock, time for a drink. But he has to leave. Depressed, he slumps in her old leather armchair, neck bare as if he were expecting to be knighted or beheaded, hands folded between his knees. She frowns—as if examining him through a magnifying glass. At last she says, "Steve Braverman, please? Steve? Am I right you feel bad that you're not intensely in love with me this afternoon?"

Oh, my God, she's smart! He looks up at her, stunned—because, now that she's said it, he knows that's exactly what he was feeling. A little gray, a little empty—and that can't be permitted, it's got to be continually intense, he's got to be out of his mind in love or he can't justify, even a little, this insanity. There's a shrewd side to Heather. Sometimes, sometimes, she seems the calmer, the older. He suspects that Heather needs him but doesn't love him.

The balance is shifting. She wanted him; he was the cautious one, fearful—let's be straight about this—that she was threatening him and could wreck his career. Now he needs her more than she needs him.

He's never been a drinker, but now, the afternoons he sees Heather, he has a drink, sometimes two; days he doesn't see her, he finds himself drinking, too. One evening as they're cleaning up from dinner, Deborah stops, takes his arm, says, "It's nice, a before-dinner drink. But an after-dinner drink? Are you sure you want that?"

It's all she has to say. He hardly drinks in front of Deborah after that. They have wine at table, wine for Friday night Kiddush. But if he gets home first, he takes a nip out of the bottle of Jack Daniels, maybe a second nip, maybe a third.

Heather is the one thing he can't talk about with Deborah—yet all he wants to talk about. Used to telling her everything, he's barely able to talk to her at all without telling of Heather first. Sometimes he describes her as one good student among several. He criticizes her as overly clever, but he's clever enough himself not to highlight her. Once she asks, "What's she like, this Heather?"

"Rather pretty. Blonde. Dates one of the other students."

"You and your pretty students," Deborah laughs.

"I don't want to destroy your marriage," Heather says to him after they make love. But saying this, her face is completely peaceful. She's in control. She strokes his flanks.

He exaggerates: "Maybe you have destroyed it."

"Steve," she says very quietly. "No, not me, honey. *I* haven't."

Steve is respected as a good teacher. This term he's growing a little sloppy in his undergraduate course—not bothering to prepare. Well, he's taught the fiction of Lawrence and Joyce, Woolf and Conrad, so often that he can wing it. But papers, which he's always made a point to get back to students in a week, begin to pile up or get hurriedly corrected. Embarrassed, he sweeps undone work under a mental rug. He doesn't just "think about" Heather; she's in every breath.

Do they know at school? He catches looks from students, from other faculty, looks he might be misinterpreting out of guilt. But then Sylvia, the administrative assistant for the graduate program, speaks to him as he's pouring morning coffee from the carafe she keeps full. "Steve?" she says. "I'm sure it's nothing. You know how grad students talk. But. . . ."

That's all. "Thanks," he says.

Ragged, one Saturday morning, he realizes that since Deborah thinks he's at the gym, he can slip away. It's a good time to see Heather. She's been complaining that he compartmentalizes her—what is she supposed to do, she asks, when he's with his wife?

But parking just across the street from her building, he realizes how unfair it is, just walking in on her. So he calls from the car. "Are you free? Would you like it if I stopped by?" "Is everything all right, Steve?" "Fine, fine." "Of course stop by. How nice. Give me a few minutes."

So he waits in his car and just when he's ready to go up to see her, the time it would take his car to have started off in Cambridge and gotten here, the downstairs door opens and a young man comes out, a man Steve recognizes—one of the students in the MFA program, older than most, early thirties. The young man, Walter something, a man with curly black hair like Steve's own at that age, hurries up the block. Steve crosses the street and buzzes. Of course, it's possible that this is where Walter lives, or where some friend of Walter's lives. He's sure neither is the case.

He doesn't know what he'll say. But something—he can't let it go. His heart is beating dangerously. He imagines having a heart attack on the stairs and being lifted on a gurney and taken to the hospital, and Deborah asking the nurse, *Where did you find my husband?* Heather stands at the top of the stairs in an iridescent green exercise suit. "Well, hi. You're here so fast."

"I saw Walter," he says simply.

"Mmm. He stayed over," she says simply.

"I see. I thought we had an understanding."

"We didn't."

"I thought . . . I imagined stupid things. I know I'm getting to be a damn fool about you. I thought maybe we could take a trip to Paris next month. I could invent a conference—"

Heather puts a finger to his lips and takes his hand. They walk inside. She's made tea. He's wearing slacks and a blazer for the synagogue, and she helps him out of his blazer, takes off his tie. He goes into a cupboard and finds his bottle of bourbon and spikes the tea. She's being very sweet to him. Tender. Tears come to his eyes. She licks them away.

"What do you expect?" she says. She sits beside him and puts her arms around him. "How often are you available to me? What am I supposed to do when you're not around? I have friends. And Steve, sweet as it's been, dear as you are, you're . . . well, honey, a different generation."

"Of course," he says, but feels his heart sink in his chest. "I know that. You imagine I don't know that? But do you think I'm going to just go away? I'm not going to go away. It's *not* going to end like this."

"Please," she says. "I want us to be friends, I even want us to be lovers. But Steve, I won't be harassed. I will stop that from happening, Steve."

"That's really funny. I thought *I* was the one being harassed. Remember?"

"Have I been hard on you, have I been hard on your marriage? The last thing I want is to hurt you."

All this time, these months, Steve has been living an ordinary life in Cambridge, sometimes making love with Deborah, feeling tenderness toward her—tenderness clouded by shame—cooking dinner with her, calling their adult children, preparing his classes, seeing their friends. Most of the time when he's alone with Deborah, he forgets Heather for hours, then longing for her washes over him and he feels crazy. He's two people.

When Heather stops seeing him, he drinks hard one night at a sports bar on Mass Ave., but next night doesn't feel like taking a single drink. Maybe he's not going to become a drunk after all.

Afraid she'll go to see the department chair—a new chair, Phil

Benzies, a colleague who's never liked him—afraid she'll even call Alan—Dean Bayer—he stays away, doesn't phone. But often for half an hour he sits on the climbing structure or on a swing in the little park across the street, watching her window, watching the front entrance, needing to give himself that pain, like tonguing a cavity. Once, while he's sitting on a swing, Walter comes up the steps and Steve watches and waits till the lights in Heather's apartment dim.

Just before the end of classes, she calls his cell. "Why have you been ignoring me?"

Her voice, its nasality, grates on him. The irritation surprises him. "Ignoring you? Oh, please, Heather. You know you're turning things around."

"You really *hurt* me," she says. "I can hardly do my work."

"Did Walter drop you?"

"No. You mean the way *you* dropped me? As it happens, *I* dropped *Walter*. That's not the point. Can you stop by tomorrow?"

"It won't be easy. Isn't it best this way?"

"I'll expect you in the late afternoon. *Please, Steve?*" She hangs up.

He's supposed to chair a committee meeting the next afternoon; he claims a medical appointment, and buys flowers for Heather, roses, a bouquet. On the drive to Heather's, he gets a call from Deborah. "Honey?" Music in her voice, something not said. "Will you be home early?"

"Absolutely. The meeting will be over by five."

"Good. I'll expect you for dinner at six. Don't be late, all right, Steve?"

Up the steps to the outside glass door. He buzzes. The hall is unlit, and so the glass serves as a dark mirror. Maybe it's because he isn't prepared to look at himself or maybe it's his own awful projection into this strange image, but he sees someone he doesn't know, face lined like a cowboy's, eyes tired. *Old.*

Heather buzzes him in. Climbing the stairs he lugs the heft of his body—as if lifting weights. There, at the top of the stairs, this shining, golden girl. He stops on the landing, heaves a breath, climbs to her and kisses her, wraps his arms around her, put his rough to her tender cheek.

"Poor sweetie," she says. "Are you tired? Been a long day?"—as if this were a marriage.

All at once, a prophet, he sees a possible future: he'll back away; she'll need him. He'll come to her; she'll keep him at a distance. He'll never know her. What he knows is the fact of the gaps between them: he old, she young; he Jewish, she Christian. It's difference posing as mystery. It's no good at all. He giggles, remembering *The Blue Angel*: Emil Jannings as the wretched professor, crumbling, in thrall to Marlene Dietrich as Lola.

"What are you laughing at?" For suddenly he explodes into laughter—his belly hurts. He has to sit down and double over to bear it.

"At *me*. I'm so funny. Hey—can a guy get some tea around here?" The thing is, he tells himself, he doesn't have to relive Emil Jannings's role. No.

He knows what he has to do.

When she returns, he helps with her big silver tray, and she says, "I know you don't mean to ignore me." And putting down the tray, he says, flat out, "Heather! Ignore you? Of course not. I've made a decision. I'm going to leave Deborah. We'll be together."

Now she stops pouring tea; she looks at him, puzzled.

"You were right, Heather. Age doesn't have to matter all that much," he says. He goes to her and enfolds her in his arms.

"Did I say that?"

"I can take early retirement. I'll move wherever you get a job after you have your PhD."

"Stop. Steve, *stop*. You're going much too fast for me."

"It'll be awful. For both of us. I know that. Leaving Deborah. The kids will think I'm out of my mind. But they're grown up. Of course . . . I'd want you to convert. Or at least try. You can take instruction from a rabbi. We'll see what happens. And I'll help you get a job, Heather. You know that, right? Whether we stay together or not, I'll help. I can't make promises, but I do have contacts all over the country."

Undermining love, *meaning* to undermine love, he holds her—maybe, he thinks, for the last time, how sad—holds her while (he's sure) she considers what he can *do* for her. Well, he can—even in this difficult year he can help. And wasn't that in the back of her mind all along? Or the front of her mind? Though longing for her in his blood, in the tips of his fingers, longing even as he plays this role, absorbing the odor of her perfume into his chest, he whispers, "I have maybe ten good years ahead of me, and then—well—you'll only be forty."

Forty! That does it. Holding her, he feels her instantly stiffen, pull back—oh, infinitesimally. He thinks how lovely it is to hold her. He wants her to pull back—it's just what he wants, just what he plotted. But doesn't he also truly want her to throw away her thirties on him?—throw herself off the cliff and he, too, fall off the cliff and fly—and leave Deborah (whom he loves especially now that he's utterly betrayed her)—doesn't he partly *mean* it—*it's crazy, it shows how crazy I am, I actually want to give myself to you*. But, thank God, it can't happen. He strokes her hair.

She's already gone.

She's gone, and, leaving her apartment after she says the words she's supposed to say, words he knew she'd say—how sweet, etcetera, of course it wouldn't work, etcetera, and he, words of how he completely understands, etcetera—afterwards, he feels the emptiness of late afternoon and feels cheap for what he's done, for who he is. He wants a drink but makes himself face bleakness. Why did Deborah call, insist he not be late? What does she know? Are we in for a terrible time? He drives across the Charles.

Deborah is wearing a new blue apron over a . . . cocktail dress. A sexy, black cocktail dress in the middle of the week? The dining room table is set for a dinner for four, and candles are already lit, though it's not dark yet. Oh, the rich cooking smells! What is it? It's lamb. Deborah, hands on her hips, leans back and laughs at his bewilderment. "It's for your birthday, dummy!"

"My birthday? That's not till Friday."

"I know, dear, but Max and Ellie couldn't come on Friday, and they're our oldest friends. They knew us when! Besides, Friday, I want you all to myself."

Sitting in his easy chair he takes the glass of wine she hands him. Steve feels old, old. Another few years, he'll retire. Already he feels the futility of keeping up-to-date in scholarship. He's got his own take on literature, understandings developed over forty years of study. But he cares little about publishing. So he feels something of a fraud in his work as well as in his marriage.

The Fleischmans arrive with gifts and party hats. The four of them eat stuffed grape leaves and drink champagne. The odors of a rack of lamb float through the room. Steve is shamed into leaving his bleakness behind. He smiles; he sighs; he smiles. Max and Ellie present Steve a caricature in pen and ink—Steve as old Jewish peddler carrying a bag of the world's troubles on his back. Steve feels tears welling up. He wishes the cartoon were accurate and he were that old peddler, simply a decent man, wishes the bag really held the world's sorrow. But no—it's just his own garbage. The champagne makes him want to open up the bag and spill it out before them, the garbage, even makes him almost believe that everyone would understand.

But of course nobody, nobody would understand.

"Thank you," he says to Max, to Ellie, to Deborah. He looks up at Deborah, for the moment awash in love. Deborah has placed little candles on the mantle, on all the windowsills. It's just dark enough for the candles to make a difference.

6

READING TO JACOB

Every night he reads to his beloved dead brother. Reads poetry, reads stories, and, accompanying himself clumsily on guitar, sings Jacob's own songs to him. The odd thing about this is that Michael is a nonbeliever. Or no: he's a believer all right—but in *nothing*—he has certainty that there is nothing beyond or within the material world. The material world is not a veil masking a deeper reality. It's just what is. Not that Michael believes only in what we can *see*. He believes in a world best explained by impossible-to-see quantum mechanics and string theory, best described by equations—problematic, quirky, even irrational. He was a double major at Cornell—marketing and physics. Now he's a successful businessman and a confirmed skeptic. However strange the world might be, it is not holy, not partaking of *spirit*, whatever that word means. And when we die, we die. Jacob is dead. That's it, and he's sure. He's *sure*. Michael mourns, he weeps when he can't stop himself—only when he's not observed. But he doesn't want to lie to himself. There are no bridges to another world and no other world to reach.

So why read to a nonexistent Jacob? And why, before he goes to bed, does he sit on the end of his bed across from the. . . ."memory shelf" (as he calls it so he can't accuse himself of considering it an altar) and talk to Jacob's picture and read to his brother, who he knows can't hear him. Michael has never particularly liked poetry, yet every day Michael reads aloud, reads Jacob's favorites, reads Yeats, reads Donne, reads Whitman, reads Lawrence.

Michael and Jacob were always close, very close. From the time they were little children—Michael the older by three years—they loved each other—and loved to battle. But only with words. And each would have been upset if the other had given in, changed his position. It was sparring, play fighting. As an adult Jacob played the contemplative, ingenuous one, in touch with spirit. He would, if Michael was there to observe, put his hands on the trunk of a tree, and draw energy from the earth or pass negative energy into the earth. And Michael would roll his eyes. "Jacob! What's your theory about this tree thing? You think it's got magical powers or something?"

Jacob hit back his brother's serve—"This maple tree? Well kind of actually. I'm kind of respectful of trees. A tree is energy turned into bark and leaves and such, a pretty damn magical process you gotta admit, but Mike, it's not a question of *trees*. There's energy everywhere. All around us. Me, too, I'm energy going in, energy going out, changing and changing. We're made of it—of energy. You took physics. Energy can never be lost. Right? 'Conservation of energy.' Like when we die, we just change forms. So I lift up my hands to the tree and I touch this eternal energy. *Adonoy echad*: God is One."

Michael didn't believe that for a moment. He still doesn't. Jacob is conflating different meanings of energy. When Jacob says *energy* he doesn't mean the energy of the physicist; it's energy seen by mystics. Isn't it enough, this amazing world of ours, without all that claptrap about holiness and God? Ah, give your brother a break.

Jacob felt the Divine Presence around him. He sang about it in his songs. He raised his hands, palms up, as if to gather it in and offer it to Michael. "God? God is always there. Whispering through the claptrap. This amazing world is grounded in God," Jacob said, looking around him as if everywhere he could see the signature of

God. "It throbs with God. Like a divine pulse. If you're quiet, you can hear. Ahh, Mikey. You—you just pretend to be a materialist."

"Why is *materialist* a dirty word? A sailboat is a material thing, but it makes you feel free. Now, that's the kind of spirituality I can understand."

Michael, older by three years, has been, financially, a lot more successful than Jacob, who struggled to get by as opening act on the tours of the famous, as "recording artist" making a pittance, in spite of great reviews; from solo gigs at small clubs and the sale of CDs or downloads. Michael was also more wealthy than their parents—their father, Nathan, their mother, Naomi—Naomi Schulman the head of the language department at Newton North High, Nathan Schulman a professor of Judaic studies at Brandeis. Not a problem. Their dad didn't at all mind that he drove a used Prius while Michael drove a BMW. Michael had, by thirty-three, built and sold a business, was growing another. Nathan, Naomi, Jacob, cheered.

And then one night, between sets, Jacob took a breather out the back door of the small Boston club where he was playing, wearing an embroidered blousy pirate shirt his girlfriend had made for him, a pretty shirt he used on stage. He was sharing a beer with his bass player when a couple of nasty drunks came down the alley and started heckling, putting him down. "Yo! Faggot in that faggot shirt. You come here and blow me."

Jacob waved them away and headed for the back door of the club. The bass player, a big guy, wasn't going to take shit. He pulled out a long-bladed knife. "Please, Danny, put that away," Jacob said. "Let's get back inside."

The bass player backed away, waving the blade side to side. They were almost to the door when one of the drunks pulled a gun tucked in his belt and shot twice—one shot hitting Danny in the belly. He dropped, bunched over, screaming. Jacob tried to get inside but the two guys charged, and he was shoved to the ground and kicked in the head, kicked again and again. They took turns and he was unconscious. Danny, the bass player, was writhing in pain.

"C'mon, c'mon!"—guy with a gun said. And they ran down the alley. Now the club's bouncer came out and, seeing what was happening, dialed 911, took off his shirt and wrapped it around Jacob's head.

Jacob lived for three days. Before he dropped into a coma, he mumbled to his brother, "Michael? I'm not going to die, am I? I feel like I'm sometimes in another world."

"Don't be an idiot. Another world! You'll be fine."

But he wasn't fine. A cerebral hemorrhage no one anticipated, and he was gone.

Now comes the grieving. Nathan and Naomi and Michael comforting and taking comfort, though there is no comfort. It's spring in Boston; the trees are blooming. That only makes it harder. After the funeral, for almost a week they sit shiva in the family home, mirrors covered. The first night, Rabbi Fogel comes to the house to lead a service. He knows Jacob well—has known both Michael and Jacob as children, officiated at the big Conservative synagogue when they became bar mitzvah. Friends, family speak. It seems like group therapy. Michael doesn't want to talk. He doesn't want to cry.

But the next morning, the next night, it's a very different rabbi, Rabbi Alter, who comes to the house. He leads services, says little. A peculiar, dark figure, not old, maybe forty, forty-five, the rabbi of a tiny basement shul and house of study—a *shtiebel*. He seems to Michael the last rabbi on earth to have inspired his passionate brother. The nephew of a well-known rabbi in Brooklyn, who leads a minor Hasidic sect—unlike this uncle he has little charisma and less of a congregation. Yet Jacob had grown close to him. He used to tell Michael about Rabbi Alter. And knowing that the rabbi was important to Jacob, Nathan Schulman, himself perfectly capable of leading a service, permits R. Alter to lead. Nathan sits holding Naomi's hand—two children, eyes closed, hardly paying attention to the quiet chanting.

Jacob, singer-songwriter of love songs human and divine, used to attend, when he was in town, Rabbi Alter's side-street *shtiebel* in Brookline—with its small congregation of men, only men. Mostly in black. Now, after the family has stopped sitting shiva, Michael attends one weekday morning. It's not a question of belief. Michael simply wants to get it right, somehow, for his beautiful dead brother—though Jacob won't know one way or the other. At the shtiebel he attends morning service and says Kaddish. He's not the only one saying Kaddish.

The shtiebel, little shul and house of study, is in a basement room with rough reading desks hammered together out of recycled, oiled wood by one of the men who prayed and studied there, with some wooden chairs, some folding chairs, a beautiful, tarnished lamp from the remains of a synagogue in Prague hanging from the ceiling, wire stapled down the wall. Light in the rest of the room is from sickly yellow energy-saving bulbs. It's a small room, cement-block with a painted cement post in the middle, an ark with two small Torah scrolls, wooden shelves with shabby commentaries and chumashim given them by a big synagogue updating editions, a leather-bound set of Talmud in Hebrew and Aramaic with English translation. Rabbi Benjamin Alter—in the dim light of the narrow basement windows at head level, the man is gray as his beard, matter-of-fact, drab, slight, eyes cast down, quiet to the point of seeming depressed; he wears a black gabardine coat, a black fedora over his yarmulke. He's mildly asthmatic, and the asthma seems like a condition of his being, as if to breathe in this world were problematic. A belt separates his upper from nether parts. That, at any rate, is how Jacob once explained it to Michael, kind of amused. And he seems so separate from other people.

He looks at Michael for a moment, then looks away. Why did Jacob think this guy was so holy? And now Michael is amused: the rabbi's polyester coat is so clean and pressed, the beard trimmed and with no crumbs of food. Meaning, for Michael, that Alter doesn't even have the crumples and grease stains of imagined Old World wonder-rabbis.

Even Jacob, Michael remembers, was a little embarrassed by all the black. "But it's a custom, Mikey. And Rabbi Alter doesn't mind if I get more colorful. Rabbi Alter, he's the real thing. You see it when he smiles at you."

But Rabbi Alter doesn't smile.

So why does Michael come back? He's busy, especially mornings, and not only for his work. He and his parents have to dismantle Jacob's rented apartment and to store or take his things. Michael takes a few shirts that feel like Jacob to him, takes a pair of worn sneakers, photos, Beatles CDs, a T-shirt advertising Jacob's own music. He takes a notebook with the lyrics of half-written songs, a cassette recorder with Jacob humming melodies. He takes a few well-thumbed books.

So much to do, and he's so filled with the absence of Jacob. Still, he drives to the shtiebel on weekday mornings when Rabbi Alter leads a minyan. Standing, feet together, trying to read the Aramaic smoothly, he recites the Mourners' Kaddish.

Some nights Michael and his fiancée, Renee, have dinner with his parents. Renee wants to be a part of their life, especially now, to offer comfort, though she's often too busy to join him. She's on a state senator's staff part time and studying at the Kennedy School of Government for a master's in public policy. To see his parents is to amplify his pain, to bring his mourning to a higher pitch, but he needs them and they need him.

One night when Renee is there and he's washing dishes while she straightens the dining room, he catches her standing in the doorway and staring at him, and he realizes—*oh!*—*I've been talking aloud to myself, and she's been hearing.* "Hey!" he laughs. "I'm not crazy, Renee. It's just that sometimes, especially lately," he says, lifting his hands in surrender, "I talk to myself. Okay?"

"I know. I know, honey. But Michael, this is different. Do you realize you're *not* just talking to *yourself*? You're talking to *Jacob*." She waits for him to take this in. "And Michael? Sometimes it's like Jacob is talking back to you. It's his voice talking. I remember his voice. You imitate him. There's a dialogue."

"It's just a hard time, honey. Like, you won't believe this. Know where I went this morning? To services. I've been going. Not just on Shabbat."

"You went with your father? To services at Brandeis?"

"No. To that little guy in black who led services here."

Back home alone in his apartment in the South End, he examines the pile of books on the side table by his bed and chooses what to read to Jacob. Is it Rumi tonight? Or Szymborska? A short story by Chekhov? What's your pleasure, Jacob? He sits at the end of his bed across from the memory shelf. So foolish, to think—*if* that's what he thinks—he can channel Jacob by this reading. Jacob would laugh, *Read for yourself, Michael. What do* **you** *want to read?* But this way of reading to Jacob soothes Michael. It makes him read very differently. It's not that the gap disappears—the gap between the living and the dead. If anything, it makes him look down dizzily into the gap—it's bigger than the Grand Canyon.

He tries reading a chapter from *Walden*—reads in Jacob's own voice. Since Renee made him aware, he's been hearing that voice of Jacob's. Because Jacob loved words, because he wrote songs and poems, Michael can hear just how Jacob's voice would sound, reading. The rhythm of his speech. And then the reading turns to conversation.

I saw your friend Rabbi Alter. I said Kaddish for you again this morning.
That's great. The big secret, brother, is that the Kaddish is for **you**.
Don't you think I know that?

But does he know that? Is it true? He thinks—for *me*? For *me*? Next morning Michael goes back to the shtiebel in Brookline— between service and driving he loses an hour and a half of his morning. Maybe that's why he does it—to give up something for his brother, not do mourning by rote.

He notices that again he's the tenth man. The day before, the day before that, he'd been the last to arrive; today, he was one of the first—but each day, without him there'd have been no minyan. He mumbles as much of the text as he can—he was good in Hebrew as a child, but oh, it's just sound now. He really doesn't know much of what he's praying. Yesterday one of the younger men led services; this morning the rabbi is leading—murmuring, murmuring.

What the hell am I doing here? I'm being so phony. Michael's disgusted with himself. But as the congregation chants the Shema, he finds himself heaving hot breath and tears, as if tears were burning in his chest. And he can't stop. He keeps his face turned from the others, he wipes his cheeks with quick motions of the back of his hand. But the rabbi sees. Michael sees that he sees. Now he feels shame, as if he's weeping in order to impress Rabbi Alter.

The service goes on; he collects himself. Last night he practiced saying the Mourners' Kaddish. This morning he recites it smoothly, as if he suddenly understood the Aramaic. He glances across the page to the translation . . . *May His great name grow exalted . . . Blessed, praised, glorified, exalted, mighty, upraised and lauded . . .* What can all that mean? It's not even about the dead—about his lost brother. But he finds himself hungry to speak the words.

Michael removes and folds away his tallis, hangs it on the rack. He thanks the rabbi and turns to leave. Rabbi Alter says, out of the blue, "Michael? I think when you weep, you're weeping not just for your beloved brother, may his memory be for a blessing."

"Oh?" Michael's hackles go up. "You're saying it's for me, then? For myself?"

"I wonder. Do you see?"

"Rabbi? You saying that maybe—well, maybe I'm mourning an empty place in myself?"

"That I can't know. I can't know that. Forgive me for being so direct, but I feel I know you. When I see you, I see your brother."

"Oh! We're so different, me and Jacob. You wouldn't believe. Jacob was so good. So much better than me."

The rabbi doesn't answer. Michael takes this *as* an answer. He's annoyed. *What am I doing this for? To hell with him.* He vows not to return. *I don't need that guy's judgment.*

But two days later, he does return. He tells himself, well, it's for Jacob.

It's a Thursday. On Mondays and Thursdays they chant three passages from the parashah of the week. A congregant comes up to bless the Torah for each passage. Today, Michael is the third.

He stumbles over the blessing; it doesn't matter. The rabbi drones Torah so that the words stream together: pure sound. Not that Michael would understand the Hebrew if Rabbi Alter chanted it like some great cantor. Michael's mind floats off and off.

Somehow, in the gap, he's aware that he's aware of the presence of Jacob. Jacob is not in one single place in the shtiebel; but he's really *here*. Michael *knows*. Oh, not that he's present as a ghost, a spirit in pants and shirt. No. Simply, he's here. Michael closes his eyes. He thinks of this as absolute craziness, it's grief talking. *God, I do need help.* But he doesn't want to lose it, this presence, crazy or no.

Jacob, Jacob.

No Jacob, of course, during the rest of the day—his time at work. He's busy; it's not till nine thirty he can get home with a couple of slices of pizza. In his apartment, protected from anyone overhearing, Michael sits on the end of the bed and talks to Jacob. Not that Jacob is present as he was at the shtiebel. Michael asks,

"What kind of brother are you?

What are you doing to me?

Are you doing?

Are you?"

"Read to me," Michael's Jacob whispers. "Read me a psalm."

"You say that because you know that the psalms are hard for me to swallow. You know I don't have faith."

"Ahh. Read."

Jacob, who isn't there, whose presence isn't even invoked by his memory shelf, just laughs—of course only in Michael's head. Michael sits across from the shelf and reads.

When he returns to the shtiebel the following week, he's wearing Jacob's favorite shirt—not the pirate shirt Jacob sometimes wore on stage and wore the night he was beaten, but the light blue silk shirt with broad open collar he wore the last few years on family occasions. In the car Michael has left a business suit, a shirt and tie, for when he goes to his office.

During the service he tries to make the Hebrew words invoke

the spirit of Jacob. Of course nothing happens—nothing. Jacob's absent. He knows better. It's a dreary, dusty room with a bunch of religious guys, some in black, some in jeans, praying. Only when he gives up all attempt to contact Jacob and, along with the rabbi chants what he can of the eighteen blessings of the Amidah, and when, along with one other man, he recites the Mourners' Kaddish, recites it for its own sake, not as magic spell but as testament, only then does Jacob slowly come to Michael. No—not exactly "come"—Jacob simply permeates the room again. He's in the musty smell of old books. Michael senses him in the odors of the room, in sweat and mold, in the dust caught in two parallelograms of sunlight that come down into the shtiebel through the dirty basement windows. Michael opens his hands and, in a sense, touches his brother. Well, *something* hovers between his hands; there's warmth in his fingers and on his cheeks. He wouldn't dare say any of this to the rabbi; he'd be ashamed. It would sound like sorcery, witchcraft, which is, Michael remembers, cursed in Torah. *May his memory be for a blessing* implies that he's gone—*as much according to Torah as for a skeptic like me*. He's here only in memory.

He doesn't want to leave the shtiebel after services, doesn't want to go to work. If this is where Jacob is most present, this is where Michael wants to be. A young boy, surely one of the rabbi's many children, comes in and puts scattered prayer books on a shelf, then goes off to school. A young man in black sits murmuring, barely audibly, in singsong, a passage of, maybe, Talmud.

What am I doing here? When I'm so busy downtown.

The rabbi stands by Michael and puts a hand on his shoulder. "The Kaddish, you should know, it's not just for *you*. It may comfort you, but it's not just therapy. Some say that for the first eleven months, when you recite Kaddish you are giving comfort to the soul of your departed; after, that soul can win you favor in heaven. Do you believe that?"

"No. Not at all. Sorry, Rabbi."

"No, you don't believe. I know. That's all right. Belief doesn't matter."

"Rabbi? I have to tell you—I've been sensing his presence, Jacob's presence." He waves his hand in the air. "Here, right here."

"That's good, that's good," the rabbi says, and finally smiles— smiles at Michael. Jacob was right. It's unexpected. A loving smile. Michael stares; does the rabbi notice?

The rabbi goes to his office at the back of the shtiebel. Michael isn't ready to leave. As an excuse for staying, he finds pail and sponge in the cement-block bathroom, finds a ladder, cleaners, and paper towels, and, before he goes to work, he washes, rinses, and dries the two basement windows and puts the ladder back. He does it as unobtrusively as he can, then puts away the cleaning supplies. He looks at what he's done and is pleased. Through the window, above on the street, a tree in its last days of flowering.

Now he goes to the rabbi's office. "I just want to thank you for morning services. The Kaddish—see, I don't believe it, what it's saying, but it turns out to speak to me. It catches me in the chest," he says, thumping, thumping. "But I notice," he says, "you've got barely enough to make a minyan—just ten men, including me. We've been lucky the past few days. If you like, e-mail me your contact list, I'll make calls to build up your minyan. I'm a pretty good organizer. It's my way of paying you back."

The rabbi reaches into a drawer and stirs the papers within. He comes up with a two-page handwritten list. "Active congregants," he says, handing it to Michael. "And men who study here. Not so active except for ones I've starred. I'm not good at making calls. Thank you."

"I'll scan the list into my computer."

"Perhaps you'd like to learn with us?—I teach Talmud Wednesday evenings."

"Rabbi—what we were talking about the other day. About some missing part of myself? It was alive in Jacob. That's what I need to learn. I don't think it's something you can teach in a class."

"I'm calling for Rabbi Alter. My name is Michael Schulman. We need you whenever you can make it in the morning for services. Seven thirty. But even part of the service—a few minutes—would be great. I need to say Kaddish—others, too. We'd really, really appreciate."

Again and again and again for half an hour.

Renee sits at her computer in his living room. When he's done, when he comes to sit by her, bringing her a glass of wine as guilt offering, she says, "Mike? You don't expect me to cut my hair and wear a wig?"

"Oh, Renee. You know I'm not like that."

"Oh—I do know. I'm joking. But lately I've been wondering. Michael dear, you're acting out of grief. You've been a little strange. You know. *Reading* to someone who's dead? Don't get me wrong: I dearly love you—I love your devotion to your brother. But should I be worried?"

Should she?

Next morning there are twelve at minyan; the next morning, fifteen. As services begin, the rabbi simply nods to Michael in acknowledgment. *It's not a question of belief,* Michael says and says again. Then of what is it a question? As the men unstrap their tefillin, Rabbi Alter reads quickly through a few psalms. From the facing page Michael whispers the English translation to Jacob. *I search for You, / my soul thirsts for You, / my body yearns for You, / as a parched and thirsty land that has no water.*

And he gets it. Oh.

Tonight, alone, Michael sits across from his memory shelf and reads a few psalms to Jacob. He reads tonight with a whole heart. "You see, Jacob, it's not a question of faith. I understand. The psalmist has plenty of faith—sometimes so much you want to say, Stop, enough already! But he's a troubled guy, this psalmist. Like me, brother, often in fear and anguish. We haven't got the Word. All we've got is our longing.

"The psalmist is hungry for justice. *Why,* he asks, *do you hide Your face from me?* Or why, he asks, do the wicked triumph? *I saw the wicked at ease* . . . It's true. It's true. *Lawlessness enwraps them as a mantle.* The wicked run from the alley, leaving you to die. You, Jacob, now you lie beneath the ground, while your killers go free. How can we handle that, you and I?"

Michael reads to Jacob of pain, he reads words of longing—the longing of someone long ago, yet not so different from now, from himself.

Not so different from you, Jacob.

Here, Jacob.

Let me read to you our longing.

7

STRAPS AND BOXES

He's speaking to the Holy One, as he does every day—every day, same time, sunrise, same station—kind of a one-way radio; not so hot on the satisfaction scale, still half-asleep he is, wearing tefillin, straps on his arm ending in a box on the bicep, and above his forehead another little black box, leather straps dangling, and in both boxes passages from Torah, reminding him of the mitzvot and of the unity of God. God is One but Harry is not—Harry is split into many pieces that rub against one another producing static in the leather boxes of the radio. So probably nothing gets through, but he keeps at it, rain or sun, summer and winter. This is me again, God, come in. Maybe this doesn't open communication, but sometimes—sometimes it does seem to open his own heart.

And it's a heart in need of opening, of opening to life. But whose isn't? Moses pleads with the people Israel to circumcise their hearts. But here's a guy, Dr. Harry Charnov, who practices psychotherapy, whose job it is to lay bare the hearts of sufferers, and yet who feels his own heart constricted, dulled. He can listen to his patients with shrewdness, even with compassion, but he, mostly, feels a little lost; feels, well, a grayness—and this is the fall, a fall of great colors in the Berkshires. He merely acknowledges the beauty. He is gray, a Jew lost "among the nations."

And then one day, this very day of my first sentence, late fall, God comes to him, speaks in the form of a shiver that ripples through him and—he's almost sure—*means* something. I could say he feels a surge of energy reaching from the box on his arm through the box above his forehead and down through him to his toes, but he himself can't say exactly what happens in his body. He finds himself in tears.

This is probably a purely neurological event, even the start of a nervous breakdown, not an encounter with the holy. At least that's what I'd think if it happened to me. No burning bush, no heavenly chariot. But for Harry it's a nudge from God—the Shekinah, the Divine Presence, brushing her soft Self against his skin. Holy goose bumps. Does he hear himself called—*Harry, Harry . . .* ? He isn't sure. He answers anyway, *Hineni,* Here I am.

I envy—even if it is, Godforbid, a nervous breakdown, still I envy. I'm as tired as Harry of this listening-for. What can I expect?—a brand-new set of receptors to pick up the music of the spheres—song of the friction, like bow on strings, sphere of the moon against sphere of the planets, sphere of the planets rubbing sphere of the fixed stars? No, no. The cold sublime of space is not the point. I want, before I die and return my borrowed materials to the sacred library, to hear whisperings of the God of Abraham, the God of Isaac, the God of Jacob. I want to draw close in love.

This longing is my enemy. I know that. Give it up, fool—here's one thing you surely can't control. Trying to control it, you lose it. But sometimes—sometimes words appear, whole sentences, and they do it for me. I can't imagine where they're coming from. They belong to someone else. They're not holy, but maybe they point to the holy? Harry listens in for the Holy One, I listen in to Harry. He wants to believe he's got a two-way connection, not something he'd admit to, secret even from himself. He wants to translate into speech what God expressed this morning in the language of bodily energies. I'm hoping he can make it.

Me, I'm an old guy with no expectations of being touched by the Shekinah. I need Harry to help me. Harry Charnov is young, mid-thirties, I see him with curly black hair, chiseled face with a beard, blue-black, always in need of a shave. He's a therapist with a private practice, works half-time in a clinic in Pittsfield. His wife, Julia, is soft-faced, pretty; she teaches high school English near

Stockbridge. They've got a nine-year-old boy, Sam. For Sam, for Julia, Harry's heart is open. How long before the grayness settles over them, too?

Julia and Harry both grew up secular Jews. A couple of years ago they agreed to join a synagogue in the Berkshires to give their son a spiritual home—that typical, peculiar move of Jews who, though not religious, are uneasy to see their children grow up without a Jewish education. But then, a year ago, Harry began to be observant. At first he was nudged by Julia: how can you make a Jewish man of our son when you yourself know so little? So a couple of times he attended services Saturday mornings. He couldn't read the Hebrew; the translations were bad, abstract poetry, and, he reported to Julia, the ideas seemed like fairy tales, psychological defenses.

Then one morning the gabbai asked him to come up to the bima and carry the Torah scroll, wrapped in velvet and silver, through the aisles of the synagogue. He had to be careful—it was like holding a baby. As congregants touched the scroll with the knotted fringes of their tallises or their prayer books, then kissed fringes or books, it was as if their tenderness and reverence altered the scroll, charged it with power. He was holding not a baby but an ancient living being in his arms. When he and the rabbi and the gabbai returned with the scroll to the bima, he found himself trembling. Still, back in his seat he felt annoyed by his own sentimentality. All right—this reverence for a scroll is ancient; the father of my father's father, he thought, must have carried a duplicate of this scroll down the aisle of a synagogue in Odessa. But what right do I have to these tears? What can it mean to me?

Nevertheless, the next week he went back, and the next. If he was ashamed of doing something absurd, he was more ashamed, he told himself, of being a broken link in a chain of parents and children going back thousands of years. It's as if he were outside this man who wept—wept because he held a parchment scroll. What a strange man that was! He found himself hungry to *be* that man. It's a little like falling in love with someone who makes no sense for your life and yet you can't stop yourself, don't want to stop yourself. Soon, it wasn't enough to carry the Torah; he wanted to say a blessing, wanted to learn to read the words as, he knew, his grandfather had done, his great-grandfather. He wanted to reclaim Torah. So he learned first the letters, then, with the help of a teacher, the words.

He came to a midweek morning minyan to say Kaddish for his father, a service where most of the men wore tefillin. So medieval, he thought. But, curious, he made an appointment with Rabbi Kohl. What's this with the straps and boxes? The rabbi showed him how to put on tefillin. And soon, though it made no sense to him, he ordered his own tallis and a set of tefillin—why not?—and put them on to daven every morning.

That's how it began—for Harry, for me.

Take away my heart of stone and give me a heart of flesh. There are moments, even before the morning God maybe comes to him, when his heart does seem to soften, become flesh. So he davens, tallis over shoulders, straps of his tefillin biting into his arm, dangling from his forehead.

This is something Julia can't make head or tails of. She wanted him to learn, not to become obsessed. Tefillin! Even their rabbi, Rabbi Kohl, doesn't wear tefillin.

Harry asks how she can possibly know that. They're only worn on weekdays.

In Brooklyn, she's heard, the Hasidim from Chabad drive a van through the streets spotting secular Jews and offering to put tefillin on them. But nobody they know wears tefillin.

Harry and Julia live in a little Christian town in the Berkshires. Three or four Jewish families. There's a Jewish lawyer on the Board of Selectmen, a Jewish doctor on the Board of Health. Anti-Semitism isn't an issue. The kids get along. They're invited to Christmas parties, invite Sam's friends over for Hanukah. On Passover they are part of a seder in Great Barrington—always along with Christians who seem to love it. But why make waves? She'd prefer that the neighbors not see, through the window of his study, Harry wearing medieval straps and boxes.

She knows better than to fight it. But it distances her from him. The closer to God, the further from Julia. In the summer sometimes she can smell the leather on his skin. Now, early November, it's too cool to smell the tefillin, but they're still annoying. "At least keep the blinds drawn." He likes the light. The sun's pretty far south in the sky and early mornings comes slanting in through green of vine and conifer, the last red and yellow leaves, moist light trapped in amber air.

Their son, Sam, comes home with a request for his dad. The fifth-grade teacher, Mrs. O'Neil, wonders would Dr. Charnov mind coming to class one day? They're exploring world religions. Mr. Shahid is coming in to talk about the Islamic faith. It would be just lovely if Dr. Charnov would do a kind of show-and-tell on Judaism.

Harry's embarrassed. He knows how little he knows. But he writes a note for Sam to take, says yes, then goes on line to find books in the regional library system. *What Jews Believe. The Jewish Book of Why.* He spends evenings reading. He wants to make it clear and simple.

He packs his tallis bag, his bag of tefillin. "No!" she says. "No! You're not going to do *that*, are you? To wear those things in class? I swear to God they'll think you're a witch doctor."

Harry should laugh, to make a joke out of it. He could say, *Hey. My patients already think I'm a witch doctor.* It's funny, Harry. Anyway, be honest: you know you'll feel strange bound in tefillin in a classroom in front of twenty fifth-graders. But Harry wants to blame Julia, and he's in a hurry to get to his office—an appointment before the show-and-tell. He's not amused, he tightens against Julia, won't look her way. This tightness—this is grayness. It's sad.

As it turns out, yes, the kids think it's weird—but interesting-weird, magical-weird. He tells them a few great stories from Torah—the patriarchs, Moses and Passover, Sinai and the golden calf. He tells them about Shabbat and the High Holy Days. Hey. It's their Bible, too. "It's just that you kids also have another one." Mrs. O'Neil—well, it turns out her father's mother was Jewish. Harry sees that Sam squirms when his dad straps on tefillin. Harry blames Julia for the squirming.

Of course, no unexpected spiritual or neurological events occur in front of the class; of course he feels uneasy wearing holy objects in this big, fluorescent-lit room with the steel-casement windows and vinyl floors, maybe trembles a little as he kisses the boxes and demonstrates their use. If he'd grown up this way it would be a different matter. He kisses the boxes and winds the straps around their cases. The kids ask questions. He tells them about the words from Torah written in tiny letters, rolled up in compartments in the boxes. Then, off the cuff, he also uses metaphors of a radio, of an energy cell connecting him to God. Here's where he gets into trouble.

It's harder than he expected. He's talking metaphor, the kids are literalists. Ricky, friend and neighbor of Sam's, asks can he touch the boxes? Will he get a buzz? Ricky lives across the street and around the corner. Harry's watched him grow from babyhood. A sweet, sweet boy. Touching, Ricky thinks he feels something weird. No, no, Ricky, it's a *symbol* of a connection, Harry says. You know what that means? It's about binding yourself to the mitzvot, the commandments. Binding yourself to God. So you can't expect . . . But then a girl touches and gives a little shriek and the velvet case almost drops onto the vinyl floor.

He's relieved to be out of there—*Thank you, Dr. Charnov, we've learned so much*—back to his office and the ordinary care of suffering patients. Things you can talk about. Maybe, he thinks, maybe Julia was right, and he calls her cell to leave a message of conciliation—"Hey. Honey? It was harder than I expected. You were right. I wouldn't do it again. But the kids were interested."

Sure, the kids were interested. Sam's friend Ricky has dinner with them and asks about "those straps and boxes." Ricky says, "I felt them. They felt weird." Harry is very sorry he brought the tefillin to class. That night he gets two calls from mothers. They're almost duplicates: *Thank you for explaining Judaism to the class. It was so kind of you. But those straps and boxes—Ella thinks they're like . . . magic. I've tried to tell her . . .*

He doesn't mind. He laughs with the mothers. *You know kids . . .* But a father calls, Tommy's father—and Harry's face grows hot with anger. *This is Joe Ferguson. I'm just curious, Dr. Charnov. What did you tell the kids today about Christianity? Did you really say they were the same thing—Judaism, Christianity? I'm sure you didn't say that.*

If you were sure, Mr. Ferguson, you wouldn't have called. No, I didn't *say that.*

And you didn't *say you had a radio to God?*

In a few days they're both aware, Harry and Julia, that something's wrong. It's a small town. Everybody living here awhile knows everybody—at least knows them to wave. You know them from library committee or Board of Health or a town or county travel team. Harry coached a junior basketball league team last year. But now Mrs. Patterson, chair of the Library Committee, seems to avoid his eyes as she walks into the organic produce market just outside of the town center while he's walking out. And Julia says that Helen Bond was stiff, seemed awfully peculiar, when they met at the gas station.

No one has invited them to a Christmas party this year except the medical director at the clinic where Harry works half-time as a therapist.

Me, I hadn't expected this to happen. I'd thought Julia would learn that most people in America are charmed by cultural differences. I'd thought she had a mistaken notion about anti-Semitism that comes from her grandparents, her mother's parents, who barely survived the Holocaust in Budapest—survived only because the Russians came in so fast that the Germans didn't have time to deport most of the Jews to the camps. *Wait,* Grandma said to Julia over and over when she was a child. *You'll see . . . You have to be careful.* A mistaken notion, I'd tell Julia.

But one afternoon Sam overhears a whispered comment in the hall outside the gym—*Look, the Jew is coming.*

When Sam tells him, Harry is wild. He wants to call and rage at every parent from Sam's class. *It's the parents are the problem.* Julia calms him. *I should never have left New York City,* he says to himself. But though he asks Sam every day, he doesn't hear anything more.

"Was I a fool to think that a Jew living in a Christian culture could be welcomed?"

"We're welcomed enough," Julia says. "They aren't throwing

stones at our windows. There are no Cossacks preparing pogroms for us. We should be thankful we're accepted as Americans."

"I want us to be welcomed—*not* as just 'Americans' but as Jews—American Jews."

"Are we all that Jewish?" She goes back to the kitchen to bake cookies for a class Christmas party. Of course Mrs. O'Neil calls it a "holiday" party, and all the images are secular: Santa and Rudolph, a snowman in the orchard behind the school, strings of lights and in the classroom windows sleighs coated with gold glitter.

No matter how you cut it, it's still ham.

Mornings, when he dons tallis and tefillin, are different now: he closes the blinds so the neighbors have nothing to see. As he prays, *Baruch Sh'amar v'haya ha-olam* (Blessed is the One Who spoke, and all world and time came into being) he holds open the blinds with two fingers, opens enough to see the snow come down. Snow lends everything beauty—cars and lampposts, their neighbors' bushes with Christmas lights shining through a white coating. It enters him in silence, enters *like* silence. No, not exactly in silence: blood hums in his ears. His breath slows.

In the gap at breath's end and before the next breath, the Holy One is present.

He stays silent and the Holy One speaks, not in words. *Holy / One:* both an appellation and pun: speaks, and world comes into being as *one, holy.* Look: here is the web of world. Evident in snow especially—details merge, snow connects. Everything past the window is conjoined with his skin, with music of the blood humming in his ears. It's not a shiver. There's an expansion: the scope of his being is enlarged so that he's out beyond the walls of his house as much as inside. Is there such a difference, inside, outside? *It's like fractals,* he thinks. The counterintuitive discovery of fractal geometry: the pattern of the large and pattern of the small are in deep harmony—

The relation of branch to limb, limb to trunk // the relation of tree to copse and copse to forest; consonance between the larger world and the world inside: the perfect mathematics of creation. And so, too, Harry's heart // the heart of the world.

This morning a kid whispering *Jew* doesn't seem like a big deal.

As he davens the Shema Kolenu (Hear our voice), he offers a petitionary prayer that his neighbors in the hill town accept his family, accept them as Jews; it is in our differences that we are one. He prays that he and Julia can love one another in the light of their differences. He goes on to pray for strength for Jim Carvel, a patient whose wife is dying young. Petitionary prayer, except for moral strength or an open heart, makes him uneasy. If God can answer, why, over the centuries, has God not seemed to answer? If God can't answer, why pray?

But this very day Jim Carvel, last patient of the day, whose wife has cancer everywhere, finally weeps in his office. Rain after drought. And Harry, who's not a toucher, a patter, gets up from his chair to touch the man's shoulder and hand him a tissue. Jim says at last what he hasn't said for all these weeks. Harry breathes heavily with the weight of Jim's pain, yet is relieved for him. Thank God. Then after, when Harry goes shopping for dinner and bumps into two parents from Sam's classroom, they don't avoid one another's eyes—they stop, each of them, to talk about their kids, talk about Christmas and Hanukah. But the odd thing is not that everything seems back to normal—an answer to this morning's prayer; it's that he feels this peculiar . . . energy humming through him, so richly that he's a little embarrassed: can Timothy's mother, Christine's father feel the energy? He finds it hard to concentrate on what they're saying. He has the really crazy idea that (not knowing it) they're bathing in this energy. He's with them, but also lifted up, above the fluorescent-lit aisle of Stop and Shop, above talk of a blizzard, and while part of him is vibrating and warm, another part is calm and cool, detached; he watches himself volley the conversation.

When he prays, he imagines that he is receiving a direct emanation of the Divine Presence, the Shekinah, though the content of the communication is blurred. At moments it's as if the world seems to be a film negative looking for a positive print. *Maybe I'm going slightly crazy.* But if so, it's not a terrible crazy; it does seem to be making more strands of connection to those around him. When he comes home tonight, he and Julia hold each other for a long time. "It's all right," she whispers. "If you want to wear those tefillin, okay. I started all this." She laughs, she kisses his rough cheek.

There are people in whose presence you are subtly transformed. Remember Masaccio's painting of St. Peter healing the sick? St. Peter doesn't *do* anything but walk past a line of sick men. Does he bless them? It doesn't seem so. As he passes, his shadow falls on them, and the ones he's already passed are now standing, the one directly in his shadow next to be healed. The people I'm talking about, they let you become for a few minutes the truest, most loving, most righteous person you can be. How do they do this? Maybe it's that they look at you—and it's not a con—with full assurance of your goodness—as simple as that. Now, when Harry meets people at the clinic or in town—say, bringing Sam to school in an evening for a rehearsal—he feels them warm to him much more than they used to, and he feels a glowing. He's in touch with something that makes him a living source.

A source: a fountain. Or consider patterns in time. He imagines a funnel in hourglass shape, himself in the narrow middle. Above, flowing into him, are generations of ancestors, more and more as you go back in time. Below, flowing out from him, generations to come. His child, maybe children; their children and theirs; more and more. Grains of sand, stars in the sky. He is a conduit between past and future as he is a single instance of a pattern seen in galaxies and inside his own blood. Patterns of the One.

At the class (let's call it what it is) *Christmas* party, the tension he felt after Sam was labeled "the Jew" has dissipated. He doesn't mind singing carols—in fact, he's always liked them—and no one looks at him or Julia or Sam strangely. He finds it easy enough to talk to the other parents. It's a big class; beside the children there are about forty adults present. As he wanders, he has the mad notion that they're basking in the hum, the glow, he feels so often now. After the homemade musical in which Sam plays King Wenceslas, Harry is drawn aside by Tommy's father. Joe Ferguson, the man who insinuated that Harry was corrupting his son's mind, puts out a hand. "Harry? I'm sorry I called like that. I had no right. My son didn't understand."

Harry pours them both a cup of fruit punch. As he crosses the "Big Room"—the gym used also for sings, plays, and parties—he becomes aware of areas of high energy, low energy. Is this just fantasy? Maybe, but he's sure he can detect energy flowing outward from particular places in the room. It's as if Harry perceives laser beams connecting the parents. Harry doesn't see but experiences lines of connection. All through the Big Room he is aware of lines upon lines, an imagined sociogram of filaments connecting everyone, children, parents, Mrs. O'Neil. Hasn't he always been aware of this web of energy? On a table in the corner of the Big Room is a ball of kite string used to block off a reserved seating section for the play. He laughs to himself, remembering an old gag: at a party, as a grad student at Columbia, he picked up a ball of kite string and handed one end to a young woman he was interested in. "Will you hold this, Ellie? It's an experiment. Hold it lightly." She did, and he unwound the string, person to person. "Here—would you hold this?" Around and around the room—"Hold this, please?"—until there was no more string. After awhile, of course, the string got dropped, dropped, dropped—could have tripped someone. It snaked along the floor, got tangled in legs and stepped on by boots, till Harry rolled it up. Tonight, tempted to repeat, he plays with the string only in his mind.

The next day after work, going to his study to check e-mail, he sees that his tefillin bag is strangely shaped, lumpy. The straps have been wound up in a jumble, the tefillin stuffed into the bag. "Sam! Sam, will you come here a moment?"

"We were just looking. We couldn't figure out how to wind up the straps."

"It's okay. But please"—he holds up the bag—"you leave this alone, Sam. It's sacred stuff. And," he adds, "it's . . . like spiritual technology—would you mess around with my new camera without asking?"

"It's just that Ricky had a bad headache so I thought it would be good."

"It doesn't work that way, Sam. It's not magic."

"Well, but the headache went away. It did. Like, right away."

"That's not holy power, Sam. It's just suggestion. As if you used a magic wand. Or a sugar pill. You understand?" He'll have to begin locking up the tefillin in the drawer of his desk.

Ricky's mother calls. "Of course I don't believe the boxes and straps you put on Ricky—"

"—That was Sam did that. Sorry. I'm going to keep them locked up. I'm sorry, Ellen."

"No, you don't understand. Ricky often has headaches lately. They can be really bad. This was the first thing that ever worked."

"It's not supposed to work like that. That's not what tefillin do. They connect you to God."

Still, he lets Ricky come over the next day and helps him take the tefillin out of the gold-embossed black cases and strap them on head and arm. Ricky's a small kid, and the black boxes seem weirdly outsized for him. Harry's uneasy, you can imagine. As a therapist he knows about "flight into health," the way a patient, before having worked through his issues, feels stronger, clearer suddenly. You don't buy it. It's always fake—avoidance. But Ricky's not his patient. What harm? He decides to talk to Ricky's mother about counseling—maybe the kid is stressed out.

Three of them in his study—Harry, Sam, and Ricky. Julia, correcting papers in the dining room, wants nothing to do with this business. Harry is sure that if a rabbi were to see this performance, he'd slap palm to forehead—*veys mir!* Harry recites the blessings for tefillin, though it's not even the proper time of day. Ricky closes his eyes. "I can feel it."

"Feel what?" Sam asks.

Ricky feels a buzz in his head and "right through me." It feels warm and nice, Ricky says. Okay, Harry says, I'm glad. Now, that's it, okay, Ricky? Harry pats the boy on his shoulder, helps him unwind the straps around his arm. It's the box strapped to his head that surprises Harry: it's more than warm; it's hot. Does the boy have a fever? No, his forehead is cool. Harry doesn't speak of this. He roughs up Ricky's hair, and Ricky grins. When the boy walks home and Sam goes into the kitchen to help his mother cook, Harry stays in his study and puts on just the tefillin for the head. The straps dangle down. Automatically, the appropriate prayer—

in Hebrew—drifts through him: *From your wisdom, O God on high, may you imbue me; from Your understanding give me understanding* . . . At the same time, what happens suddenly is not understanding but a jolt of electric pain through his head—pain and heat—and he plucks off the tefillin, feels it with his fingertips, looks and looks at it, wraps the straps around the box and puts both head and arm tefillin away in their green velvet bag.

After dinner, Harry calls Ellen Corbett, Ricky's mom, and walks the few hundred yards to her house down the middle of the narrow street, new snow piled up on both sides. She's recently divorced, single parent to Ricky and Catherine, back to her maiden name. He knows that Julia wants him to stay away from dangerous ground: other people's children, not to mention attractive single mothers. Sam remembers when Ricky and Sam were six months old, when they splashed as infants at the YMCA pool in Pittsfield.

Ellen lets him in the back way—he doesn't want Ricky to know he's here. Look, he tells Ellen, it's probably nothing, but just suppose the headaches . . . and suppose the tefillin . . . Ricky's up in his room; Ellen hands Harry a cup of tea. He tells her about the pain, the heat. "I don't know what it means. But suppose Ricky is really sick."

The tumor is large but, blessedly, benign. The pressure is gone, the headaches are gone. Medical magic—though of course Ricky is a little woozy, Ellen is still scared. Who wouldn't be? The day after Ricky comes home from the hospital, Harry, Julia, and Sam bring over soup and a salad. Once Julia becomes involved in their lives, she begins to consider Ellen a potential friend. Surprising them, Ricky is able to come to the table for dinner. He looks weak—he's lost weight and was always a skinny kid. Ellen is quiet but happy, grateful. Tears well up.

Ellen promises to keep the story to herself, but when he gets back to school Ricky lets out hints of what happened. The children tell their parents, the parents tell friends, and soon everyone in town seems to know that some kind of "Jewish magic" was at work. This way of seeing the story disturbs Harry, disturbs Julia. It's the flip side to medieval whispers of well poisoning. Twice the next month—now it's February—patients come for an initial consultation but before the hour's up Harry sees they're not there for psychotherapy but for magical healing. Sam comes home with a rumor that just *touching* Dr. Charnov will heal anyone. Of course, nobody *believes* it, not exactly *believes*, but now when he goes to the library or the produce market, townspeople don't avoid his eyes; the opposite—they smile, they shake hands. No one says a word about his *powers*.

So? Does he *have* powers? Not him, not *Harry*, thinks Harry. As he is an hourglass funnel from generation to generations, here again he is a conduit.

What's happening, you'll probably say, is that I need to give him powers, use him, a key to a door in myself, to my own heart. Maybe so. The story has turned the tefillin, a signpost meant to bind us to the Holy One, into a set of magic boxes, amulets that can draw down power and light.

Harry is bewildered.

He wears tefillin only when he prays in the morning. But often, though he can look to his left arm or touch the spot above his forehead and know there's nothing there, he feels certain that he has strapped on tefillin. He wonders: are there inner tefillin as there is a secret Torah? As he walks through the world—at a party, or the synagogue's social hall during Kiddush, or the dead streets of Pittsfield, its downtown a cemetery of empty stores, the natural foods market in Great Barrington catering especially to weekend New Yorkers—he's aware, through inner-whispers, almost-images, in a dreamlike knowing, of this person's life, that person's life.

As a therapist he "hears" people's secret stories more than he ever has. It's not magic; it's listening with a third ear, seeing with a third eye. That doesn't mean he can help a patient drop habits of defense, dead practices no longer needed, but it's a start. At home he seems to know Sam more deeply. He *gets* Julia. Watching her correct essays at the kitchen table, he finds himself loving the nape of her neck, loving the way lamplight makes her light brown hair glow. And he feels in his own neck the way she judges herself, almost sees Julia's mother, arms folded, standing over her, dissatisfied.

He finds himself becoming more tender to them. That's good.

But elsewhere, the tenderness he feels is a burden, too much responsibility—he can't bear it: to walk through a potluck dinner and hear the music of this one's pain, that one's pain. It's as if he's tuning into whispers in a language he doesn't quite understand, so that all he gets is the music of pain and of keeping pain at bay. He feels Ellen Corbett's loneliness, knows she's walking a tightrope, afraid to look down. He sees her life. Day by day, she holds it together: works, rushes home to make dinner for Ricky and Catherine, takes care of things around the house, does it all again the next day. It takes a large martini to douse Harry's awareness.

In synagogue he senses he's being observed, spoken about. Gossip about "healing" must have made its way to the synagogue. Synagogue buddies look at him strangely. He gets calls from Jews, men he knows from synagogue, Jews who have never touched tefillin. He deflects—as a therapist he's learned to deflect—"Tell me what makes this so interesting to you"—playing the question back to them. But some of the calls are not so pleasant. "You don't think the goyim have enough stupid stories to tell about us?"

What am I to do? Dear God, what do you want to tell me? Do I really want to hear?

Does he want to hear? Maybe not. It's too much for him. Now he hides everything strange from Julia. When he bumps into an acquaintance, he keeps a transparent barrier between them. He davens in the morning but stays outside the words, keeps them words. At basketball practice he stays cheerful, talks town politics, makes jokes. And the whisperings dim, and he's grateful. Because he doesn't feed it, because he acts "normal," the story runs its course.

And it's sad but maybe necessary: the inner whispering, the music of people's lives, quiets. He's pushed it out, he's deafened himself to this music. And perhaps because he's blocked it out, Harry has also lost the strange intimations he calls *God's whisperings*.

Sad—but mostly he's relieved. *Come in, this is Harry again,* he says each morning as he puts on tefillin when he prays alone in his study, facing the mizrach, the ornamental plaque marking the East, with a stylized image of Jerusalem. But it's okay there's no holy trembling, no nudge from the Holy One. He goes about his prayer business. It's a loss, sure. The glow that went with the tefillin for a while, the presence of the Shekinah, they belong . . . to a tale. Harry is back to living a life of small joys and annoyances; more than a little of the old grayness has returned. The hero has dissolved into the story Harry told, and Harry is once again just a Jew lost "among the nations." He has been stripped of his peculiar relationship to sacred gesture.

His gesture is lost to me, too.

What are we to do?

Sometimes, especially when he prays, Harry is aware, as we all are, of invisible fibers linking him, say, to Sam, getting dressed in his bedroom, to Julia fixing breakfast in the kitchen, and filtering out through walls which are, after all, mostly nothing—emptiness surrounding form. Patterned energy: shaped Nothing. And his heart—for it does feel like his heart—seems to have lost its integuments somewhere, which is good, and now, if this isn't wishful thinking (Harry's, mine) perhaps his heart, more bare, is a little better able to expand to touch Julia and Sam, to touch his friend the lawyer past the next crossroads, Ellen Corbett across the street. To touch Rabbi Kohl in Pittsfield and Henry Dowell, five miles up the road. A fiber of thought reaches down the hill, up another and along a ridge to Mrs. O'Neil, till a giant web, ultimately woven, Harry thinks, by the Heart of the world, begins to form an invisible net over the Berkshires, draped from steeple to steeple, cell tower to cell tower. It connects people—and not only people: what about the deer that made it through hunting season, what about the birds at our feeder? Attuned to this secret web, by spring, while there's no magic left, he feels less gray. Attuned to Harry, I feel less gray. I'm wary of coating these hills in a fairy tale of wholeness, wary of making up a story to protect me, to enliven me, but, breathing in, I'm aware of the same web Harry touches, pulsing, pulsing.

8

His hand has its slight tremor as he holds the razor under his chin. He's as careful with it as if it were a straight razor. Well, he *has* nicked himself a few times. Croft washes off the soap with scalding water and investigates his reddened face in the enlarging mirror— not out of vanity, God knows, though he's considered a handsome man, youthful for fifty, his face sculpted like Scott Fitzgerald's before Fitzgerald bloated up. Not vanity—he wants to know if he's missed spots, if he looks "seedy." Naomi said to him one night last fall he was "beginning to look seedy" and said it gently, *not* to hurt him. So he's careful. He dresses in perfectly creased, quite new, expensive wool slacks, a fine cotton pale-blue shirt, a paisley tie his daughter Jenna bought him, a cashmere blazer.

Coffee's ready. Stuart Croft adds sugar and half a jigger—vodka to avoid detection. Not that he's been drinking all that much lately. But can he help a little nervousness? It's such a cultural ritual—a father taking a son to look at colleges. He simply wants to appear *capable*, he tells himself as he folds a handkerchief into his breast pocket the way his own father folded one every day of his life, last thing before he'd walk out the door every morning; then Dad would grin at Stuart and Tim, and *"There!"* Every morning until the morning he walked out the door for good.

"There," Stuart says now and pats his jacket for his keys. Would it be worthwhile to bring along a couple of rackets, a couple of cans of balls? No—he wants Michael to see this adventure as something serious. So, Burberry over his arm, overnight bag in the other hand, he's out the door.

Winding his way off the Expressway to the North End, he calls Naomi, and by the time he's at her block of condos she's there to let his car in. The electric gate slides shut behind his car.

Michael, tall, with black curly hair from Naomi's side of the family, wears a jacket with a little patch, logo of the boarding school he attends. No tie? Well, we'll see about that, Stuart thinks. For interviews he can wear one of mine.

White walls and chestnut beams from when these condos were warehouses. It's the first time he's visited her since she moved from the rental on Beacon Hill. Naomi has fixed up the condo beautifully. It's not cluttered with furniture. He recognizes some of her favorite pieces from their house. From what *was* their house. He feels superfluous here. Is it always this neat, he wonders, or is it for my benefit? Oiled wood and white walls, plenty of light. It's full of morning light; the living room looks out on Boston Harbor.

He beams at Naomi, absolutely glows with all the comic, raised-brow charm he can muster at nine in the morning. Naomi takes his arm, stretches up, and kisses his cheek. He likes her hair like this, her not-lawyer hairdo—wild, long; she's in jeans and turtleneck like some bohemian out of mid-twentieth-century Greenwich Village. As if she knows what he's thinking, she combs her fingers through her hair. "I'm playing hooky till noon. No clients. Would you like coffee before you go? You'll be careful driving? I know you'll both be perfectly fine . . . You'll take care of our boy?"

Take care of our boy? Stuart pretends it's a joke, offers his reassuring smile, the smile that always makes him feel strong and competent. Wouldn't you buy stocks from this smile? It's his father's smile: his father, who held a seat on the New York Stock Exchange, a seat he'd inherited from his own father. Now brother Tim is the broker in the family, not on his own but for Morgan Stanley. Stuart has always been the maverick in the family. Marrying a Jew, getting a doctorate in literature, divorcing, he's grateful he's had permission (trust fund, intellectual interests) to be the maverick, off the hook—teach part time, write part time—let Tim uphold the honor of the family.

He hasn't told Tim and Annie he's making this trip; they'd want to see their nephew on the way through New York. Stuart wants to be a little selfish, have Mike to himself for three days. The past years, with Michael away at school, he's rarely seen him for three days at a time. Well. They did fly to Wimbledon last year for the championships. They skied at Vail the last couple of winters. Otherwise it's been a dinner here, an overnight there. Michael's a backpacker. Not Stuart.

Three days. Crazy, but he keeps saying to himself, *Can I hold it together three days?* It's a bit scary, as it must be for a man who's had a tough time getting it up: to worry ensures there'll be something to worry about. Stuart wishes he could honestly pray. He wishes he could take some kind of pill that would guarantee he'd have no shaky feelings—just be a good father to a splendid son.

"Well, I happen to think," he tells Michael, downshifting the BMW up the ramp of the Expressway, "this will be one fabulous trip. Now, I don't want you to feel pressured in any way—the fact that *I* went to Princeton doesn't mean . . . I've made a reservation for tonight at the St. Regis in New York. Tomorrow night, a fabulous restaurant in Princeton. Well. How does it feel, thinking about college. Excited?"

Michael buckles his seat belt and, slumping his long body down, fiddles with the radio. "*If* I even *go* to college. I'm thinking—I might defer admission, take a gap year. Please, Dad, let's not argue about it, okay? The thing is, it's like I'm tired preparing to prepare to live. Getting into *this* school so I can get into *that* school. I want to do something—I don't know—real. And big."

Stuart doesn't argue. This is a boy who begged to learn to fly at twelve, wanted to start a business when he was a first-year at prep school. Recently, Naomi tells him, he's pondered a political life. Senator Croft.

"When are you retaking the SATs?"

"Dad, I'm not trying to be difficult, but can we please not get into that?"

"—Because I would be happy to help tutor you. In everything but math."

"Actually, my SATs are perfectly okay. They're all already in the 700s."

"Right, right." After all, Stuart doesn't want to sound like his own father. All he'd talk about, the rare times he got to see him after his father remarried, was grades. When he was at the Taft School, then at Princeton, Dad would put a hundred dollars into his bank account for every "A." He was his father's employee. It wasn't the money that mattered; he never even spent the money. It was, Stuart supposes, a sign of his father's concern. Then, when he was out of school, on his own in graduate school, it's as if the camera of his father's eye was shut down. His father never understood why he wanted to study literature instead of going into finance, where, his father said, a chair was being warmed for him. He did this study on his own, and for the first time, he stumbled. This was when the pangs in the belly began. He stumbled through his graduate work, did well enough. But right there, the very start of his career, was its end. He's published, he's taught well enough, but the spark he once had—it fizzed out.

"Right, Mike. Your SATs are okay." They're silent. Mozart fills the air. Finally Stuart can't stand it. "But look, Mike. The schools you're applying to—it's your choice, but they're unbelievably competitive."

"Okay. Then you know what? I may not get in."

"Right," Stuart laughs. "Right. I'm just. . . ." Shrugging, though with a big grin pasted on his face, he tells himself, hey, does it really matter if Michael goes to Princeton? Stuart has been through all this with Dr. Klein: "Try this on," Klein said. "Are you asking Michael, because you think of yourself as a failure, to do your successful living for you?" And Klein rubs his forefinger over his lips, a gesture that's always meant to Stuart, *I could say more but I won't.* Stuart agrees but wouldn't put it that way. It's more that Michael is the only thing in the world that matters to him, his substitute for a future of his own. Of course his daughter, Jenna, too. But Jenna has *made* her life—a successful life. All he wants now is to launch Michael. All right: yes, it's true—it might make him feel like less of a bum.

Because frankly, that *is* how he feels. As a child Stuart was the star of the family; his father, even after he left, would brag about Stuart's grades—almost perfect, even at Princeton. Tim barely got through. Now Tim is the star. He, Stuart, began teaching at Tufts but never finished the book on critical theory that might have won him tenure. He teaches part time at a second-rate school.

He's glad to pass the baton.

In Providence they visit Brown; they take a campus tour and info session, and Michael attends a class in history. Stuart finds a seminar in Emily Dickinson and gets permission to sit in. While Michael goes for an interview, Stuart wanders. Young women— some blousy, overweight, unkempt, but some, oh my, young beauties. Out of reach. He remembers Naomi's hostility when he'd stare at the pretty young women on the college tour they took with Jenna eight years ago.

That's not why Naomi kicked him out last year. He was becoming a white elephant, a peculiar family appendage who arrogantly spouted opinions to her friends (aesthetic, political) in a murmured, cultured drawl, as if they weren't worth the breath. And let's admit it: the breath was often alcoholic. There was that. At times he'd work himself up (he knows now after years of therapy the game he was playing) to feeling judged and alone—so he could slip away for a weekend and do more than *look* at some young woman. Naomi is right: he wasn't much of a husband.

But he's always been a loving father.

He wonders, as he sits on a bench near the old brownstone admissions building, whether Mike is relaxed enough to shine. God knows the boy can shine. *Being with him fills me with life.* He fantasizes strolling into the interview and explaining to the admissions officer how wonderful Michael is.

Did the boy keep my tie on? Is he remembering to tell about his experience in debating?

The lawns are beginning to green. Spring flowers coming up in the beds. Lunch time. He wants to go where he can get a drink. And now from across the lawn he sees Michael, tall, beautiful the way he strides, the way he holds his head high. A girl notices him, turns her head. Stuart grins.

After lunch he's got a slight martini buzz on so he lets Michael do the driving to New Haven while he tilts back and takes a siesta. Yale's on spring break, but they attend the info session, take a student-led tour, and walk the lovely campus. Stuart can't bear to leave without showing Michael the Yale Center for British Art—though Michael warns, "I'm not crazy about painting, Dad." Stuart plays the docent, teaching Michael a bit about "British Orientalism," lecturing on Blake's illustrated books. It's as if the beautiful campus, the museum, flow into his veins and strengthen him. He's closer to feeling like his persona—well dressed, cultured, a gentleman who knows his way around.

He himself drives to New York, along the park, in spite of traffic down Fifth, to give Mike a look, though Mike has been to New York often. "You remember the Guggenheim—where we saw the Spanish show? *And on your right,*" he sings out like a tour guide, "is the Met, where your famous father escaped to after school." They pass the apartment building with the hawk's nest on an arched pediment, pass the Central Park Zoo. Pulling over at the St. Regis, he hands the keys to a doorman.

When he was a kid growing up in New York he used to see his own father at the St. Regis. After his father moved to Chicago, the St. Regis is where he'd bring his second family on trips. It's so unabashedly elegant, high ceilings, painted cornices, mirrors in ornate frames, it's almost camp. It's a museum of bourgeois luxury gone by. They exchange a sardonic look. "I wanted you to get a taste of all this rococo brocade and luxury. Still. It's also a damned nice comfortable hotel."

"But it isn't your kind of place, Dad."

"Well, thank you, Michael—I think. No, it isn't. It was my father's. We used to see him here just before Christmas."

Before dinner they take a walk through Central Park, then down Seventh Avenue into the theater district and a small Italian restaurant, Michael's favorite. The wine relaxes him, and walking up Fifth Avenue he wraps an arm over Michael's shoulder and tells him about attending openings of Broadway shows, his mother pointing out with her eyes, with her cheek, the *Times* reviewer, the theater columnist from the *New Yorker*. He wants Michael to open up, tell about his life. He doesn't know what questions to ask so it doesn't sound like an interview. After all, Christ, he doesn't even know the names of Michael's friends at school, doesn't know which sports he's playing, doesn't have a clue about what music he listens to. *Do you still listen to the Grateful Dead?*

Michael says, "I wouldn't mind living in New York, going to Columbia. Or Princeton, that would be cool—I could take the train in. I've got lots of friends in New York."

"Oh? Tell me."

"You wouldn't know them. Just friends."

They pass the Plaza and the Pulitzer Fountain where Fitzgerald once jumped in as a young man, a contract for his first book in hand, having won Zelda, knowing himself a gigantic success. "But riding in a taxi, he started crying—Fitzgerald tells the story—he'd never be this happy again."

Michael shrugs.

"What is it, Mike?"

"Nothing."

"There's something."

"Oh, Dad. You can't just come back like this and everything's suddenly all right."

"Wait a minute." He sits on the rim of the fountain. It's cold. "That's your mom talking. Who says I want to be away from you? You're off at school. What can I do?"

A long silence. Stuart tilts his head to look into Michael's eyes and show he's waiting for an answer. Finally: "You could visit."

"Frankly, I didn't think you'd want me. All right, I promise. 'From now on there'll be a change in me,'" he sings. "I'll visit. It's hard to explain, Mike. I feel afraid sometimes."

"You feel afraid?"

"Well, not exactly. More a question of *uncomfortable*. Or *not worthy*. It's actually an improvement, that I can speak about it. Your father is becoming stronger. *And*, you'll say, *about time*."

The room at the Ritz Carlton is big, with twin double beds, lights of the city twinkling through the curtains. Stuart spreads open the curtains and, one hand in his pocket, offers the city to his son. But Mike has taken out an SAT practice book—Stuart's sure it's to avoid having to talk.

"I thought you weren't retaking the SATs."

"I never said that."

Stuart feels bad for having spoken of his weakness. What son wants to hear that? Still, he's a little hurt. He shuts the curtains and yanks the drapes closed, as if Michael were unworthy of the view.

"Well, if that's your idea of fun, I'm going down to the lounge."

On his way to the elevator, he tries to soften. It's hard, living separately as we do, Michael hearing whatever he hears from his mother, it's hard. But the closed doors and soft-carpeted hall depress the hell out of him. "Hell with him," he says aloud in the empty, decorous corridor. "I'm doing my duty as a father. I'm doing what I'm supposed to be doing."

So now he considers himself off-duty.

But something grieves him; of course it's got to do with Dad. These rooms, these halls, though refurbished, bring him back to those Christmas visits—the only times he saw his father—his father, Madeline, their children. Madeline used to pull Stuart into her soft, soft, full-length mink coat; he hated how good it felt. He hated her perfume, her sympathy.

He can't blame his father that the visits were so awful. Wasn't the poor man trying to bring together the parts of his life, to make his sons feel he was still connected to them? What Stuart felt each time was that he was being evaluated. He and his brother Tim had to perform, express gratitude, show fondness for their stepmother. Tim, cynical, always more comfortable with himself, shrugged it off. But Stuart spent half an hour in front of the mirror to style his hair the way his father wanted it; he dressed in pressed pinstripe suit for luncheon at this very hotel. Now Stuart is sorry as hell he brought Mike here. What is he doing this for? Salt in a wound.

In the lounge he orders a drink, sits listening, someone's playing standards, looks at a young couple, clearly lovers, reads Richard Wilbur's translation of *Tartuffe*, orders another drink. He calls up to the room. Michael is watching some action film. "Well, don't wait up for me," Stuart tells him. "I'll get in eventually. Remember, tomorrow morning you have a ten thirty at Columbia."

After the second drink, time on his hands, he telephones Melanie Ames, who lives by the river just off Sutton Place. They used to have a thing going a couple of years back, he and Melanie, and maybe Dr. Klein would rub his fingers over his lips, narrow his eyes in concern, but it's not a sexual move, not exactly. Melanie happens to be home—she's a busy woman, a senior editor for Farrar, Straus, and doesn't gad about during the week. Understood— but will she taxi to the hotel and have a drink with him? She's dubious, it's getting late, but . . . just for a drink. Why not? She'll be right there.

And she is. Melanie looks lovely to him. Elegant, not over-jeweled. It's always been so easy to talk with her. She wears a long velvet skirt and a soft mauve blouse, and she says in her musical low voice, "What fun," and they drink martinis and talk about the translation of *Tartuffe* and the elections, and he tells her how god-awful his students are this semester, and she says, well you should see the manuscript I was working on today. They laugh and remember, and he brags about Michael, and suddenly he gets an idea, says, "Why, you've just got to meet him, he's right upstairs," and he calls Michael on cell and says he's bringing up a friend, "so look your best."

He signs the check and stumbles on his way to the elevator, and Melanie laughs and says, "Well, you haven't changed a bit, have you? Remember the tango party at the Jordans'?"

He remembers, he remembers, they had a dancing instructor and everyone was too drunk to follow. "*You* were too drunk," she says. "But always a gentleman," she adds. "Well. Five minutes and I have to get back home and to bed."

Stuart raps at the door and uses the card-key, and Michael, dressed in jeans and a T-shirt, is sitting on one of the pretty, un-comfortable chairs in the room, reading, waiting for his father. Stuart realizes this introduction thing was a big mistake, a big, stupid mistake, because he can hardly stand straight. If a cop asked him to walk a line he'd be cooked. "Michael, hi Michael, my dear Michael, this is Melanie, Melanie Ames. When you write your first novel, you send it to her."

"Do you write?" Melanie asks Michael.

"Did you want me to leave for a while, Dad?" Michael says. "I can go take a walk."

"It's nothin' like that, nothin' like that," Stuart slurs. "Just introduce you, that's all."

Next morning, that's the last thing he remembers, his saying that. He wakes hung over, not bad, rubs his eyes. Michael's gone. "Mike?" Michael's gone. "Well, son of a bitch!" He looks at his watch. Almost ten thirty. He calls Michael on cell, but there's no answer. He showers, dresses, grabs a cab, and wanders the Columbia campus. Near Low Library he spots a tour, and he trots over, but Michael's not in the crowd. The interview should be over. He feels like a fool. He walks in an angry rush through the gates onto Broadway and hails a cab.

Michael's not in the room, and his cell still doesn't answer. He leaves a message. "Michael, I'm really sorry. You should have woken me. How did the interview go? We need to get to Princeton for dinner, so I hope you're here soon. I'll be waiting. Love you, guy."

At three, Michael knocks and comes in, and behind him, Naomi. "I picked up Mom at LaGuardia," he says matter-of-factly.

"Well, Naomi."

"I'm sorry, Stuart. I told him to call me if anything like this happened."

"Like what? What happened? I got a little tipsy. Don't you know me by now?"

Naomi is dressed in a charcoal suit for her law office, her hair pinned up, her eyes cool. *We are not amused.* "Get your things, Mike." Naomi sits on one of the uncomfortable chairs and waits as Michael packs.

"Listen, Naomi, why don't you come with us to Princeton? The three of us? My treat."

"I have no time, Stuart."

"But *Princeton.* I had to work hard to get him an interview. They don't *do* interviews. Mike has an appointment with the chair of English. Fact that I got a little tight—"

"And," she says in a dry, lawyerly voice, "the fact that you brought a woman up here."

"Not for *that*. Not for *that*. Is *that* what you think? Just to show off this boy! Michael, please. I'm not that stupid. Take off a day, Naomi. We'll be there for dinner. I've got a reservation at Lahiere's. No alcohol at all. All right? No alcohol. Promise."

"Oh, Stuart." He hears her voice soften.

"Let me explain, all right? No, please." But then he doesn't know where to begin. He can't speak for weeping. He weeps, and just when he thinks he's done, he starts up again. He sits on a bed. His whole right hand masks his eyes. He feels the pressure of Naomi, who comes to sit by him on the bed. She rubs his back. He's trying to tell her he's not asking for sympathy, but every time he speaks, he falls to weeping. Now Michael sits at his other side and puts an arm over his shoulder. "I'll go with you to Princeton," Michael says. "No alcohol, you promise? Right?"

"I'll change my appointments," Naomi says. "But we have to be home tomorrow night."

They take the Lincoln Tunnel to the Jersey Turnpike. To keep up their spirits, Stuart, a tenor in an amateur chorale, sings Rodolfo's aria to Mimi from *La Bohème*. "You see?" Naomi says, sitting behind. "Your father could have been an opera singer. . . ." She adds: "A pretty ghastly one."

"It might help," Stuart says, "if you had a case of consumption. It would inspire me."

"Dad!"

"Michael, dear, you've got to understand," Naomi says, "that when your father and I make vicious digs at each other, we're at our lowest level of conflict. I mean yellow, not even orange."

Stuart, calling ahead, has found another room for Naomi. Its availability is just luck, but it feels like a personal success, and he needs all the success he can get. He tells Michael about Princeton —its preceptorial system, the eating clubs, the wonderful students.

"Of course," he says, "you only take from it what you bring to it. I didn't bring much except a quick mind. I was a pretty callow youth, young man. You're a much deeper person—I mean it."

He means it, and he fantasizes starting over again. As he squints into the sun going down, he imagines beginning again with a father who gave a damn. Without a needy mother, bitter about taking care of the two boys on her own. Maybe to have grown up in a deep way in the church they belonged to—the way Michael grew up in synagogue. At Michael's bar mitzvah, Stuart was proud of him—but ashamed how much he envied his son.

Beginning again without fear. Without alcohol. And while Michael and Naomi talk easily about sailing this summer, Stuart thinks, why *can't* I start all over? He doesn't mean, of course, going back to college. He means being somehow washed clean. He can imagine what it would feel like. Not to have to lug all his baggage around. Not to drink himself to sleep at night. Leaning back, he reaches for Naomi's hand, gives it a squeeze.

He dines without a drink. Somehow, having orchestrated this dinner, his stock has increased in value by its quality. Afterwards they walk through campus. Stuart points to memories. Michael walks slightly ahead and Stuart takes Naomi's arm. "Imagine our kid going here?" he whispers.

Their hotel, the Nassau Inn, is just off campus. Their rooms are on the same floor, and as Michael walks ahead with the key-card, Stuart smiles at Naomi and raises his brows. It's humorous, but a question, *What do you think . . . ?* asked in the most casual way possible. She pretends it's a joke, but she squeezes his arm. "You and Michael stay together," she says. "You never get a chance to spend time together—and I've got work to catch up on."

So he hangs out with Michael. The fact that Naomi is in a room just down the hall changes the music of their relationship, Stuart and Michael. It's as if she's secreted a video camera on the mantel. It makes them both behave with kindness, with generosity—they're both their best selves. Michael actually asks for help with the critical reading section of the SATs.

So they work together for nearly an hour, and at ten wash up for bed and read. Michael's reading Toni Morrison's *Beloved*, and Stuart wants to ask—is that for school? Wants to tell him Toni Morrison has taught here at Princeton, but doesn't want to interrupt the reading, doesn't want Michael to lift his eyes and sigh, *Yes, Dad?* So he reads poems by Emily Dickinson. When they turn out the light, Stuart can't sleep. For an hour he can't sleep. He'd read but doesn't want to wake Michael. He has pills for this. Maybe a small drink would be even better—but he's promised.

Slipping into chinos and a turtleneck he lets himself out. Just to take a walk. There's a lounge downstairs; he'd better keep away—just read in the lobby. On the way to the stairs, he passes Naomi's room, and just maybe she's awake and they can talk. He taps with his nails on her door. She must be asleep. He tiptoes away. As he's about to open the stairwell door Naomi opens.

"Stuart! What are you doing up?" she asks. "Couldn't sleep?"

"Did I wake you?"

"That was nice tonight. He loves you—you know that?"

She's standing in the doorway, he in the corridor, and suddenly, at the same time, they laugh—here it is, almost one in the morning, and they're ten feet apart chattering away in a public space. She puts a finger to her lips and opens the door wider to invite him in. "All I have is water," she whispers.

"I guess I'm going to need to learn to like water." They sit in ladder-backed, padded chairs turned toward each other. Such depressing chairs. Why are they depressing? They're perfectly decent, unassuming chairs; the management has even tried to make the room charming, give it a slight panache of Colonial America. They've failed; there's the bland, anonymous quality of a hotel room. But would it matter what chairs these were? Whatever they were they would absorb and reflect back the gray surface of his life. He is forced to experience the failure of his old hope that she could reach inside him and find the seed of his dormant life—like the life he's always seen in her.

His temptation is to dredge up the mistakes of last night, but he stops himself. He says, "Mike and I worked together a good hour on his SATs. The boy's smart."

"Good genes," she says.

All at once it feels simple, clear, what he wants to do: he stands up, reaches out a hand to her and helps her up. He holds her; she lets him. Her fingertips touch his cheek. But when he presses himself against her and kisses her, she turns her head. "Not now. Definitely not now. I think we both ought to get some sleep. But it was nice tonight, Stuart."

It's as if he's taken a drug. His whole body is softly aflame, and he needs to take deep breaths and let the energy flow and dissipate. "Good night, Naomi."

"We're doing pretty well on our own, me and Michael," she says.

"I know. You're amazing." The door, he thinks as he tiptoes back to his room, the door isn't closed. And in the ten seconds it takes to walk from room to room, he imagines getting sober and finishing the final chapter (for that's all he's missing) of his book on critical theory. It's been sitting there for five years. What was the sick satisfaction of not finishing? A final chapter—and some of the research brought up to date. It could be a surprising book, a fresh look at multiple voices, building on the work of Bakhtin. It's possible. It could change his life.

Once inside the dark room, he's too charged up to get to sleep. He could read in the bathroom. Instead, he unzips his toiletries, takes up the bottle of cough syrup, really a half pint of bourbon in a cough syrup bottle, and takes one long sip, another. It's like taking medicine, he thinks—not the kind of drinking he's promised to do without. Relaxed, he heads for bed. Passing Michael's bed, he looks down and blesses the boy without words.

In the morning Michael is almost silent. Stuart doesn't bother him. Michael waits till they've ordered breakfast, then says, "Let's go home after breakfast. I'm not applying here. Just so you know."

"Okay," Naomi says, vexed. "Any reason? After we drove here from New York?"

Michael says to his mother, as if they were alone at the table, "I smelled his breath. He woke me up when he came back from the lounge. I smelled him. He went out drinking last night."

"Oh, that," Naomi laughs. "No. Actually, your father came to my room, and we talked, and we had a little, very small drink together. That's all it was. Please, Michael. Please? You'll enjoy the tour. Nobody's going to make you go anywhere, you goofy boy."

Michael turns to his father solemnly. "But you *promised*." Still, Michael doesn't insist on going right home. He meets with the chair of English. He goes through the tour and information session. As they stop at the lobby of the library, Michael presses forward to hear over the echo, and Stuart whispers to Naomi thanks—thanks for covering for him. See, the little bottle of bourbon, he explains—it was medicine, really. A sip to help him sleep.

Naomi just sighs, "Oh, Stuart. Really, Stuart."

Stiffening, grim, he slips forward to hear the young woman praise Princeton's research facilities.

They're on 84 heading toward the Mass Pike. Michael's in back, reading. A Handel concerto grosso plays softly over the front speakers. Naomi, arms folded, stares out the window. It's been this way for hours except when they stopped for gas and stretched their legs. Stuart rehearses things to say, crosses them out. There's nothing to say. He wants to tell them he's going to be sober. He'll start attending AA again. But to say it means nothing. He's said it before.

They get caught up in a line of cars trying to get onto the Pike. He shuts off the music. "I don't claim to be a perfect human being." He says this almost as if speaking to himself.

In back, Michael guffaws.

"Michael!" his mother says.

"I've been a better father than my own damn father, that's for sure." He says it quietly, as if to get the record straight.

Michael breathes out an exasperated sigh. "Well, sure. *Your* father walked out on you. You—you didn't want to leave, I guess."

Stuart just nods and looks at the road. Traffic inches toward the toll booth. He sees his father all dressed up that morning the same way he dressed for business. Stuart is ashamed: he knows he wants to claim sympathy without acknowledging that he's claiming sympathy. He keeps the story of that morning running like a home movie behind his eyes. He sees his father's angry eyes. He was ten years old, so Tim must have been five and didn't know what was happening—just that his mother's yelling that morning was scary. But Stuart understood and grabbed at his father's suitcase and hugged him around the waist. *"Please don't go, Daddy." And I was crying, and he pulled my fingers apart and straightened his vest and growled, "Get out of my way, you little shit."*

At ten, he was old enough to know how awful that was, how final, how unforgivable. Also old enough to realize it wasn't really directed at him. It was Dad's way of attacking Mother.

Stuart creeps toward the tolls. His stomach is churning. He's sucked sympathy out of that story once too often. Uch! Listen! He's told it to women he slept with—slept with them using the goddamn story as one more tool. Humiliating to remember! Shameful! Which is worse—his father's ugliness or the way, these forty years since, he's sipped that ugliness? The way he's told it to *himself*, over and over—like pressing your tongue into a painful cavity. What's the satisfaction?

He takes a turnpike ticket and says nothing. It feels like being dead, the cars a line of the dead trudging toward the River Styx, the car taking him to the world of the dead. And Naomi and Mike? Along for the ride.

"Dad? Listen." Michael leans both elbows onto the back of his father's seat. "I don't think you're such a bad father. It's just that . . . I mean, you *promised*."

Naomi says to Stuart, "You're certainly *not* like that father of yours." And to Michael, "That bastard, your grandfather—his only contact was sending checks."

"He saw me now and then," Stuart says. "At Christmas. He meant well. He was who he was."

Traffic thins out, the Handel ends and *All Things Considered* comes on. They listen to the news. Naomi says, "It's good that Michael's disappointed. It shows how much you mean to him."

"Mom! Don't speak for me. I hate that. Okay? Mom?"

"People get sober," she says. "I swear to God, Stuart, I can see you doing it."

Stuart rehearses telling her, *I've been disappointing people all my life*. Why does he hunger to say this? To get her reassurance? To slacken the pressure on him in case he fails again? To garner sympathy? *Poor* Stuart. Now we're at the core of it. Uch! As if I've got a hole in the middle and the only thing I know to fill it with is self-pity. *Come, everyone, look at the hole in me!*

"I swear to God . . . ," he says. He can't finish.

9

ALL THE CHILDREN
ARE ISAAC

It's the same every morning, only more and more terrible. While David Levy does his exercises, he listens to the latest griefs over the radio. Drought has cut to less than half the livestock of some village in northern Kenya; desperate herdsmen are forced to slaughter their scrawny cattle. In Indonesia, an earthquake kills hundreds. In this country, millions lose their jobs, can't make payments on their homes. Families are forced to move in with relatives or, sometimes, live out of their cars. Yesterday NPR told of one hundred people killed by a truck bomb; the day before it was villagers found tortured and beheaded. A roadside bomb kills a soldier, a villager. Soldiers come home with brain damage, without legs. And for each of the dead or damaged, a hundred lives are turned upside down, families broken, children left without parents, parents without children.

Chaos, the chaos that engenders loss of meaning, enters the world.

Finished with his exercises, he remembers in his prayers the dead and the living. He mourns the dead and worries for the living. But why talk to God when the kind of God one can talk to is, in a sense, the problem in the first place? If he could accept a world in which things just happened, if he could acknowledge that justice is not built into a sacred patterning of things, then there'd be no point speaking to God. Suffering would be of no sacred significance.

Claire says, –David, you've been like this since we said goodbye to Sarah.

They're having breakfast together in the country kitchen they had built a few years ago in their house in Cambridge. Every day he feels the tension between this sun-filled room and the weight of suffering he carries.

–Are you saying, he asks, that only personal losses should be sufficient to account for someone's sorrow? Is that what you're telling me?

–Please! Don't be so high and mighty. Of course not. I know you too well for that. You've always grieved for everybody's sorrow. I respect that in you. But since Sarah, since Sarah's death, there's been a difference. Shouldn't I worry?

To take away the sting, Claire puts down her coffee cup and kisses his cheek.

The tragic Rabbi Nachman of Bratslav tells us that every day for an hour, we are to break our heart before God, break open and speak our pain. David cites the authority of Reb Nachman to his wife. Claire nods, she knows about Reb Nachman. She says, granting the hour of breaking open your heart, –All right, but what about the rest of the day, David? Doesn't Reb Nachman say we are required to be joyous? He lost both his sons, he lost his wife, he suffered and died young from tuberculosis, yet he told us that joy is a mitzvah.

Unlike David, Claire is not even Jewish. But she knows Nachman. She's smart, an intellectual historian at B.U. That's where David met Claire, auditing a grad course in Nietzsche that she was teaching. Judaism, Catholicism, Buddhism, she studies them not for truth content, life-truth, but for what they can tell her about believers. Is she too smart to grieve? No. He has seen her grieve.

Of course it's not Nachman's beautiful, mad vision, vision of a God before Whom we are instructed to weep, that makes David grieve, that washes over him, wave upon wave. Often, when he's by himself, he lets go, he weeps, he begs God to comfort the Afghan girls who, on their way to school, had acid thrown in their faces, flesh gouged to the bone. The men who burn with acid the faces of those girls feel justified, holy. Ideology excuses violence, justifies it even for those who have not been victimized.

Not that he suffers only for anonymous victims he hears about over the radio. What about Jim Welsh in their book group, whose MS—or is it ALS?—keeps getting more debilitating. First his wife Jane had to help him off and on with his coat; now his arms flap like empty coat sleeves at his sides, and his speech has become a gnarled whisper. Or Jennifer, David's administrative assistant, who's had one miscarriage after another.

Or Jeremy, of course; always, always there's Jeremy. Jeremy's photo is in front of him as he says morning prayers. One prayer tells him, "Serve God in joy." It doesn't say how.

Over coffee before they each leave for work, David to the importing firm he runs in downtown Boston and Claire to B.U., Claire puts a hand over his hand. –I get it. Sure. Joy is hard to come by. Honey? I feel sad losing Sarah, too. Especially after Jeremy. But David, let's be thankful for your sweet Lisa. And let's be thankful for our Danny, thankful Danny's okay.

–Don't you think I am?

She adds, –By the way, honey. Danny, he's coming for the weekend. He called.

–Danny's coming when he's so busy? Claire? Did you ask him to come?

–I always ask him. Of course.

At once David is delighted, but suspicious. Is Claire so upset about his grieving that she feels she needs to bring Danny home? Danny's finishing his dissertation in anthropology at the University of Chicago. How can he get away for a weekend? And at once David begins to worry: the plane—will the cargo be adequately inspected? He sees an explosion in the middle of the sky. And what about the air circulating in the plane? Suppose someone has flu.

Reb Nachman said, "All the world is a very narrow bridge, and the most important thing is not to fear at all." He knows it's a mistake to carry too large a load over that bridge—yet it seems that every day the load grows heavier, breath comes harder.

•••

When his first wife, Sarah, was dying last month, Claire and he flew out to California. Ostensibly, it was a trip to see Claire's sister in Santa Monica. Really it was to say goodbye, and of course, Sarah knew. It wasn't just David who needed to say goodbye. Claire, too. Over the years, Claire and Sarah had become very close. A funny thing: Sarah made Monroe—her second husband, husband of twenty-five years—keep David and Claire outside while she put on her makeup. Even dying, and she knew she was dying, she wasn't going to be seen looking awful! They stood in the garden and looked mournfully out over the lawn, over the roofs of other houses, all the way to Catalina. Then, with a paisley silk scarf around her shoulders to give her dash, another, bright golden, as a turban to cover her bare skull, Sarah was ready for them. Monroe came out to the garden to call them in. Monroe, something of a dandy, sporting a small, neat mustache, wore a maroon silk shirt streaked with ointment and liquid. Monroe, David, Claire, sat around the hospital bed Monroe had set up in their living room in Pacific Palisades, in the house Sarah had always wanted, by the plate glass window looking out over the ocean. Monroe and David, wanting to help, hovered clumsily.

Sarah rolled her eyes at Claire. –These men!

Claire laughed and shook her head.

–Claire, dear, can you fix my scarf? *At long last* I'm a good kosher wife, hair all cut off.

–You'd never know it! Claire said, as a joke, not a lie. She fixed the scarf. Taking Sarah's head between her palms, she held her cheeks, kissed the scarf on her head.

–Look at these husbands of ours, Sarah said. Running around like chickens with their heads cut off. Relax, relax, kids, I'm not going anywhere today . . . Still, still, Sarah said to Claire, her words thickened by drugs, as she fingered the plastic tube of her IV, still, these men are okay. But don't tell them, she stage-whispered. It'll go to their heads. Still . . . we've had pretty decent luck, Claire, in the husband department. Could have done a lot worse. Now she sighed. –But then . . . there are other departments. Thinking of Jeremy, David was sure, Sarah had stopped smiling. She wouldn't meet their eyes. Eyes drooping, half unaware, she plucked at the wires to the monitors, playing an inaudible music. –Monroe, dear? Can you make sure it's okay . . . down there? Her words were slurred. She pointed to the valley of blanket between her legs. Just then Lisa walked in. Their daughter, David's and Sarah's. She'd flown in from Cleveland. She was silent. Always gentle, she tiptoed to the hospital bed and kissed her mother's cheek.

Monroe lifted the sheet to take a look. –It's fine, he says. The catheter is just fine. I know it feels peculiar. But it's fine.

–You know! My big shot. If you really knew! My mother at the end used to raise her forefinger and say, "God should only destroy my enemies the way I'm destroyed." Ha ha. The trouble is, my enemy, it's my own body, that's my enemy. But whatcha gonna do? Whatcha gonna do? Good afternoon, Lisa darling. Don't look like that. Shh, sweetie! She smiled at everyone. Then, as if she realized, ahh, she didn't have to be the life of the party, she closed her eyes and slid under the opiate. David looked at her face.

Bleary. Soft as a girl's but no longer the face of a girl, as he no longer had the face of a boy. When they first met, they had been boy and girl. David's breath became deep, hot. *Decent luck in the husband department.* Sarah was letting him off the hook, telling him it was all right, all of it. Their angry marriage—when they were practically children. She was eighteen, he was twenty. She a dancer with big eyes, a junior at Barnard. He a senior at Columbia, a revolutionary with long, curly black hair—knocked around that spring by the police when, one 4 a.m., they stormed the administration building the students held. They broke his granny glasses, hauled him off to jail. Too scared to occupy the buildings herself, Sarah told him she was proud of him. Those days Sarah wore her long hair in a ponytail that trailed almost to her waist. They went to old movies, attended emergency committee meetings together, waited in line for standing room at the Metropolitan Opera. They slipped into the second acts of Broadway shows after intermission. They had pet names for each other. He read William Carlos Williams ("Asphodel, That Greeny Flower") to her. They attended demonstrations against the war in Vietnam. They were going to lead a wild, beautiful, sexual, revolutionary life. They weren't going to be trapped in bourgeois torpor. They would live passionately in an uncreated America. They would create America.

Two months after meeting, they subwayed down to City Hall and married, both of them dying to get away from their families. For god sakes, they'd neither of them ever lived away from home! How could such a marriage not self-destruct? A romantic ideology can take you only so far. They fought and fought. She became pregnant with Lisa. And that scared her. They had so little money. Sarah was still at Barnard; David took a part-time job but started grad school. Sarah stopped pretending to encourage his revolutionary ideals. Like his mother, she complained about their poverty.

David had come from a family with very little money. Money was what his parents fought about. Night after night they yelled. His father lifted his hand to slap. He never slapped, but he shoved, and his mother would crumple to the carpet in a theatrical faint. Getting up, she put out her nails to scratch.

Married, Sarah and David snarled and snapped. Or brooded, wouldn't look at each other. Sarah had never had to consider money. She was used to expensive clothes; her family traded for a new Cadillac every year. There were trips abroad. It turned out she didn't want to give that up. The romantic choice she'd made frightened her.

–Don't you *see?* she snapped. This can't be *La Bohème* anymore. It can't be romance at the barricades, I'm pregnant, and I'm a college student.

David pretended—pretended to himself—to be morally outraged. It was the ultimate betrayal. He'd expected to live in graduate-student poverty. Now, with a baby coming, he had to make money or take it from her parents, and that he couldn't stomach. Her parents were continuing to pay her tuition. That he accepted—nothing else. He dropped out of grad school, got a job, through Sarah's father, with an importer in downtown Boston, tripling his wages. They packed up and moved to Boston. How peculiar: he found he actually liked the work. And he was good at it! Still, he made Sarah pay.

All this was forty years ago. Now Lisa's son—his grandson Jeff—is entering middle school. And that afternoon last month,

Lisa, their beautiful, smart daughter, eyes shining wet, sat by her mother and stroked her hand and whispered to her, though Sarah was asleep.

Suffering in his own life, in the lives of those he loves, seems incommensurable with the suffering he hears about every morning. Those villagers, the Afghan girls. Still, suffering is suffering; loss, loss. And then, as if that weren't enough, there's the suffering we bring upon ourselves. To think how he coated with ideological veneer his fear and anger as a young husband. How we torture ourselves and those closest to us with vanities! He tortured. He openly resented Sarah for pushing him into the business world. Then he discovered that, secretly, she was taking money from her parents! He became furious. She felt entitled to the best. He felt entitled to judge her with contempt.

After Lisa, they had Jeremy. Then, wanting very different lives, they separated.

So peculiar. A strange blessing: within a year or two they were better friends than they had ever been lovers; for the next thirty-five years, brother and sister except that one terrible year when they lost Jeremy. On Thanksgivings, at Passover seders, they were almost always together, an extended family—David, Claire, and Danny, his son with Claire; Sarah and Monroe, Lisa and, when she grew up, her husband, Arthur, their son, Jeff, and Jeremy, David's son with Sarah—as long as there was a Jeremy. On and on—at least fifteen at the table extended with plywood, covered with cloths. Once upon a time.

For an hour, two, they watched Sarah sleep in the room with glass wall, lovely room looking out over the Pacific. Noises came from her throat. She woke, she slept again. Somehow, they were ashamed to look at one another—he, Sarah, Monroe, Lisa. Strange. Dying was making them ashamed of expressing anything, even grief. Especially grief. Grief they swallowed. Seeing her enmeshed in tubes and wires, pain blurred by morphine, animal sounds coming from her throat, David asked himself, as five years ago he had asked himself when Jeremy died, Is it all worth it? Dear God! The whole deal, going through life, putting your children through a life that ends this way—is it really worth it?

It's probably nothing, Dad. I'm doing acupuncture.

Have you seen a doctor?

It's nothing. Really.

When Jeremy died—in just over a month, diagnosis to death—Jeremy took the world with him. Nothing seemed beautiful. It was a dead world. David loved Claire, loved Danny and Lisa, but they couldn't take away the sense that the world was dead. He mourned not only his loss but the loss for Lisa and even more the loss for Danny, who had loved his big brother, half-brother, fiercely.

Sarah he couldn't speak to after Jeremy died, not for a whole year, and he still doesn't understand why. At the time he thought he was aggrieved because she had known, a week or two earlier than he, how sick Jeremy felt, and she hadn't told him. But that wasn't it. Maybe it's just that when he spoke to Sarah, he experienced her grief compounded with his, and it was too much to bear. Then, slowly, as the grief remained but the world returned, he was able to be her friend again. The change occurred at the unveiling of Jeremy's headstone, a year after the funeral.

Maybe—and isn't this what Claire means?—he listens to the griefs of the world not for their own sad sake but to give him justification for a priori mourning, something in which to ground, lend legitimacy to, his sorrow. If this is true—isn't that shameful? The suffering he hears about is real in itself, must be attended to for its own sake. When he hears over the radio the wife of an army sergeant, a soldier who returned home from Afghanistan with brain damage from the shock of a roadside bomb, he wants to comfort her, to help her husband get better treatment. In the end, he finds their telephone number—they live in Newton, just a few minutes from his home in Cambridge—and calls to offer sympathy and ask if she needs anything. He spends an hour on the phone, listening to her tell him how wonderful her husband had been, how much he has deteriorated—and he sends this stranger a check and gives her the name of an effective lawyer. But how many calls can he make? How many checks can he send?

●●●

Friday afternoon when David comes home early for Shabbat, Claire is working—working at the dining-room table so she can spread out around her laptop documents on the youth movement in Germany in the early twentieth century. *Der wandervogel*, groups of nature-loving youth, and their connection to later Nazi youth movements. There are Xeroxes of essays, photographs, journals—their pages held open with clips. Other documents are bookmarked on the web. He pours them glasses of white wine and sits watching her work. He leans over to kiss her forehead, smell her skin.

She hooks her hand around her neck and says, —Sit a couple of minutes. I'm just finishing.

For just a moment, looking at her taking notes, it's 1976. He walks into a graduate class at B.U. and there she is. He'd found Claire McCann's name as instructor of a graduate course and called her—might he sit in? He'd taken the few courses he needed for business. He'd been made vice president in charge of marketing at the same small import firm he got his start with. Soon he planned to start his own company. So he took courses in management, in marketing, in accounting. He had no intention of finishing an MBA. Claire's course, Nietzsche in the Context of Modern European Thought, was just for pleasure. Claire was thirty, the age of most of her students. He was pleased by her simple, lucid explanations. He was pleased by her broad mouth, open face with high cheekbones, her smart eyes. He's still pleased just to look at her. And she's still teaching him.

How funny the difference between David then, in 1976, and David eight years earlier. By 1976 he was making good money. All that conflict with Sarah over money!—and look—by now it wasn't an issue. His success made him wonder: was his drama of purity, his indifference to money, a fake? When out of the vestiges of radical identity, faithfulness to an image that had once defined him, and certainly out of irony—he would joke, I want you to know, Claire, you're sleeping with a wild-eyed socialist, she would laugh:

—It looks to me as if at least five days a week you're something of a clear-eyed capitalist. Hmm. Do you think there's a contradiction? But we'll let that go. I know you, David. What you are is a good man. He was flattered, and loved it that she was sophisticated enough to say something that simple.

Now she shuts her laptop, straightens her papers, turns to him. –Danny called from Logan, he'll be here any minute. So? Are you happy? She asks.

–Of course. You know I am. But what did you say? Did you make him think I was in a terrible state?

–He's got research to do at Widener.

–Right. Right. And there's no such thing as interlibrary loan.

–Honey, look: the thing is, don't you maybe need to see someone? Get pills prescribed? I'm talking turkey with you. It scares me. You've never been sad like this. Except of course after Jeremy . . . You, my adventure capitalist.

He takes her hand. –Thank you for your goofiness. But this isn't depression.

–Oh? Then what would you call it?

–Well, I've gotten older. I see what's up. I mourn. If someone's depressed, it means he can't find anything in the world worth loving. But the mourner has lost something he loves. Something precious. A depressed person sees nothing precious. He wants to wipe out the world. It's meaningless, worthless. His own life feels worthless. Maybe after Jeremy's death I felt that way for a time. But now, that's not me. Is that me? For instance, I love you, Claire.

Even as he says this, he knows he's sweet-talking, not being honest. Oh, what he said was true enough. But he's not acknowledging how strong the dark feeling is in him: *Dear God*, he said to himself when Sarah was lying there connected to life by tubes and wires, as he said to himself when Jeremy was lying in a coma in the ICU, *is it worth it?* To go through a life that ends this way, early or late, is it worth having life for yourself, giving it to children you love? Fool! As if there were a choice! But even then, watching this son, this young man he loved, begin to die, he didn't feel that life was worthless. It's because he so intensely wanted life for Jeremy that he grieved, that afterward he mourned. And so we say, May his memory be for a blessing. Let it be the blessing of his life we remember.

For an instant, David sees Lisa and Danny, Sarah and Monroe, sees Claire and himself, and two of Jeremy's friends, sees them as if he were a camera outside and above—all holding hands in a prayer circle just outside the ICU. He remembers Lisa starting to weep and Sarah becoming very upset at this, because to weep was to admit the possibility that Jeremy could die.

–You can't go back into his room if you're like that, Sarah said to her, to all of them. When we go back inside, you're going to tell him he'll be fine, you're getting stronger and stronger. You've got to put positive energy into that room. So David had to weep in silence. In his curtained-off section of the ICU, Jeremy lay in a coma. Just before the doctors induced the coma, Jeremy had asked in his slurred speech, –So what is this? It's so strange. Dad? I keep feeling . . . I'm at a place between worlds. Am I going to *die?*

–No, no, David said. Of course not, of course not.

Sitting by his bed, Sarah stared at her son. She stroked his head. Unconsciously she pumped her left hand with her right, as if her left hand were Jeremy's heart, as if she were keeping it going. Oh, she knew.

David began a prayer for healing in Hebrew: –*May the One who blessed Abraham, Isaac, and Jacob bless and heal . . .*

Lisa touched his hand. –Shh. Shh. You're upsetting Mom.

David didn't understand.

–Any prayer in Hebrew Mom associates with a Mourner's Kaddish. She told me Hebrew has to do with death.

–This prayer has nothing to do with the Kaddish, Lisa.

–I know. And really Mom knows. But please?

He prayed silently for healing. But he was already mourning. Afterward, for the prescribed eleven months, almost every day, he found a service at some synagogue where he could recite the Mourner's Kaddish, a praise of God in memory of someone you've lost. The minyan at synagogue was healing. For others were also in mourning. David remembered the story of the Buddha telling a mourner, a mother who asked for help with her grief, to go from door to door till she found someone who had suffered no losses. Finding no such door, perhaps she was appeased by the commonality of grief. It's almost the definition of the human. Helpless before grief, we can mourn together.

•••

Just in time for lighting Shabbat candles and making a blessing over the wine, Danny appears with computer and overnight bag. He puts away his bags. They stand at the kitchen table and David offers Shabbat blessings, then lays his hands on the head of his son and blesses him, this big, hefty son, taller, broader, by many inches than his father.

David says, –But, you, you're the real blessing. How good to have you home with us And how's Andrea? (Danny is half-living with Andrea.)

–Andrea's great. How are *you*, Dad?

–Oh, me? Okay. I can imagine what your mother has been telling you. She thinks I'm depressed.

–And? So? *Are* you depressed?

–Your mother informs me we're supposed to be joyous. It's true. Especially on Shabbat we're supposed to be joyous. That's especially easy when I see *you*.

–Well, good. I'm relieved. Sure, Mom told me you're going through stuff. But that's not the only reason I'm here. I didn't want to spoil the surprise by telling you over the phone. We need to talk about a wedding . . .

In a rush, the weight of breath eases. Now David's lungs fill with joy as irrepressible as grief. But at this moment of unexpected joy, David also knows. Knows that this beautiful son, this gift to them and gift to the future, this young man who may, please God, carry, thousands of years into the future, our genetic codes, our cultural codes, has been, since the moment of his conception, a hostage to life. And because they love him, they can't help offering him up. Until Jeremy, David hadn't really understood: All the children are Isaac. And sometimes the ram is nowhere to be found.

THE CAMERA EYE

It's July 1939; in a little over a month Hitler is to invade Poland. Half awake, Eddie Rubin shambles toward the kitchen in his old bathrobe that's getting too small for him. His mother's still asleep. Eddie smells the eggs his father is already frying up for him, crackly as the radio news—Hitler massing troops on the Polish border.

Eddie feels bad for not listening. What about those cousins on his mother's side, trapped in Berlin? But he's never met them. He's seventeen; it's the summer before his senior year in school. He's more worried about going on to college; even if he wins a Regents scholarship, he could end up like his father, selling stoves and refrigerators.

His father pops the toast and butters it for the two of them. Now Dad takes a ferocious dishtowel to the pure white surface of the new, high-end GE fridge. Dad babies that fridge like a new car, uses so much force his belly wobbles, his face gets red and damp. Funny the way he keeps doing that! The fancy fridge looks ridiculous in this shabby kitchen in this West Side walkup apartment. Rust stains in the sink, scratched, faded enamel covering the oven doors. A fridge too big for the three of them. Dad got it at cost from his boss, Sid Stone, at Stone Appliance. So right away it's become a battlefield in the family wars. His mother turns up her nose. "Naturally. He couldn't get rid of it to customers so he dumped it on you!"

Eddie stays out of it.

Dad sits kitty-corner from Eddie at the metal kitchen table and rubs the baked white enamel surface with his dish towel. When he gets worked up, he's everywhere with that towel. Years later, sitting in this kitchen after the war, grieving for the loss of his father, Eddie will remember, with that camera always working in his head, the force with which his dad rubbed away imaginary spots with a towel, will remember the heat pouring off him through his clothes.

"Looking forward to the trip tomorrow, huh? The Big Guy—Mr. Stone—he says the Hudson River Day Line's the way all the sports travel. He says we'll see a lot of big spenders on deck. 'American sports,' he calls 'em. We sail up the river, pick up the car at the train in Albany—his big sixteen-cylinder Caddy with the pull-up seats. I'll tell you a little secret: Mr. Stone thinks a lot of you."

"I got to get ready for work." Eddie takes his cup with him.

"You play your cards right, Eddie m'boy, and there'll be a place for you in the business. Who knows? Selling appliances at first. Mr. Stone might even pay your way through college. God knows I can't send you to college myself. He could just write you a goddamn check. Mr. Stone says—"

Eddie doesn't wait to hear what Mr. Stone had to say. He waves at his father, goes off to get dressed for work. Since he can remember, one of the main topics of conversation in the house has been Sid Stone—

"Sidney *Steinberg*," his mother sneers.

"So what if he changed his name to be more American," Dad says. "His father couldn't even speak English. And ain't Sid Stone a hund'r-percent American?"

"My dear," says his mother, "Sidney Steinberg is a Jew from Brooklyn who puts on the dog. He simply wants to attend the king's reception at Buckingham Palace, don't you know."

It's like a bad play, Eddie thinks—you could write what's coming next.

"Listen, he's got your number," his father says. "You're just jealous is your problem. Miss Hoity-toity."

"I'm sure a sophisticated member of the Social Register like your Sidney Steinberg"—she pronounces *berg* as *boig*—"knows everything there is to know about a woman like me."

Times like these, Eddie retreats to his room. He turns up his radio and shuts himself inside his closet, turned into a darkroom. It's a big closet; he's removed the closet bars, shoved what he could under the bed, hung clothes that needed hanging from a bar braced over the top of the closet door. He's got no air in the closet; it's probably lousy for him to breathe the chemicals. But the darkroom is home.

Stieglitz, Bresson, Evans, Lange. They've taught him how to see ordinary life. They're his teachers. They'll matter to him all his life, even after the war, after his time as an army photographer, when the life he saw was anything but ordinary.

For the summer he's got a job at a butcher shop on Columbus Avenue. Mostly, he delivers roasts and steaks to the Beresford and San Remo and Dakota—the big apartment buildings along Central Park West. Lately, though he's had no training and it's probably illegal as hell for a boy of seventeen, he's been cutting meat, especially scraps for chopped meat. Knowing the fat and gristle that goes into the grinder, he sees why his mother always makes the butcher grind meat in front of her. He's been hand-washing the same three crew-neck T-shirts for work; they're all stained with cow blood, the stains mostly bleached out till the material is soft and gauzy, hardly a shirt anymore.

Ahh, who needs a shirt? It's been one hot summer.

Tomorrow and Saturday he's been given off from Adler's Meats—to go with his dad up to the races at Saratoga. This after months of his mother rolling her eyes. "So. You think you're getting somewhere? That man wants you to carry his bags," she says.

Eddie is awakened by his father's knock early the next morning, "Let's get a move on, sonny boy," and by seven thirty they're down at Pier 21 on 42nd Street waiting for them to take the chain off the gangplank of the *Peter Stuyvesant*. Dad rocks from foot to foot, a small man with too much belly, peering between shoulders to where the taxis are letting off passengers. Hands in his pockets, leather overnight bag between his feet, he jiggles the keys in his pocket. No Sid Stone. He takes a comb out of the breast pocket of his checked sport jacket and reaches up to give one last grooming to his boy.

Eddie grabs the comb away and, laughing, runs it through his father's thinning hair.

"Okay, I get the point, I get the point. Relax—I just want you to look like a swell."

No Sid Stone. The chain comes off the gangplank, and the passengers, off to Bear Mountain or Indian Point for the day or up to Kingston or all the way to Albany for the weekend, start passing them. Dad is already sweating. His nice, new sports shirt is damp under the arms. He thumps fist into palm like an outfielder. Finally, "Here's the Big Guy himself."

As Stone steps from a cab, Dad stretches up and waves. "Here, over here," Dad calls in his big baritone that seems outsized for him. Then, to Eddie, "Ya see?"—as if he's proven something. He waves again, and Stone takes off his dove-gray fedora and holds it above and behind his head and freezes, as if someone were snapping a picture. Dad whispers to Eddie, "Why'n't you take a picture? The Big Guy would appreciate it! You take such good pictures."

Eddie leaves the Kodak around his neck.

Mr. Stone weaves through the crowd. "Come *on*," he says, says impatiently, as if it were Eddie and his dad who were late. They follow him up the forward gangplank. "Tell you what we're gonna do," Mr. Stone sings out over the noise of the crowd, hum of the engines. "We're gonna get chairs on the upper deck and watch this big sonofabitch pull out."

So they climb iron stairs past a couple of lounges to the upper deck, but all the chairs are taken. Mr. Stone is irritated. "Maybe it's for the best, Mr. Stone, Sid," Eddie's father says. "We'll stand and we'll get our sea legs."

"What the hell we need *sea* legs on the goddamn Hudson River?" Stone growls. He guffaws. "I'm making a joke, Rubin. So. This is your boy. Last time I see him. . . ." But Stone has stopped looking at Eddie. He's checking out a young lady in a long blue skirt and frilly white blouse.

Which gives Eddie a chance to look the man over. Stone has become such a big deal in their house that he wants to see for himself. Sid Stone is a handsome man in his late thirties, with strong, cleft chin, regular features, a straight nose—easy to hide the fact that he was born Jewish—taller than Dad, though shorter than Eddie himself. Not all that big really—he's got the knack of looking big. He wears his thick, black hair plastered back, parted near the middle. Fedora tilted back to indicate relaxation, he stands at the rail and, just for laughs, waves to the admiring throng on shore. "Smile for the suckers," he says. Eddie notices that he pulls in his stomach, throws back his shoulders and puffs out his chest. It's probably that woman in the white blouse he's puffing up for. Wearing brown and white wingtips, pale-beige linen slacks, precisely creased, and an off-white sports jacket, Stone looks as if he belongs in a magazine ad for an expensive car.

And this pathetic phony, with his squint-eyed, one-sided grin—*I'm smiling, but don't forget I'm shrewd*—is behind all the fights in their house! It's not just his mom that makes Eddie see Stone as phony. It's his swagger, that theatrical voice. The worst thing, for Eddie, is what the guy does to Dad—soon as Stone's around, Dad's own voice changes. And at home, Eddie realizes, when his father's voice sounds arrogant and false, he's just imitating Sid Stone.

"Some day for a trip on the river," Stone calls out through the noise of wind and engines to the pretty young woman in the white blouse. "Wouldn't you agree, Miss?" He removes his hat, tips it to her. "You traveling alone?"

She smiles vaguely—and looks the other way. Mr. Stone calls, "Oh, Miss? Miss?"—then mugs despair and pretends to eat the brim of his fedora. The gangplanks are up, the ropes are flying, the engines rev, the boat pulling back churns up the river, then turns. The big boat feels sluggish. With almost all the passengers on the starboard side, it seems to lean a little, but pretty soon, as people move around, it stabilizes. They pass the docks of the West Side. The *Queen Mary* and another liner are in port. Stone thumbs at the *Queen*—"Wouldn't it be great if I had the time to sail on that baby?" Eddie and his father follow Stone around the deck to the Jersey side. A tug pulling two loaded scows passes them, heading to Garbage Land. The Palisades come into view.

"Say, Marty, why don't you go negotiate us some coffee while I talk to your boy here."

"Cream and double sugar coming right up, Sid."

"While you're down there, find out when the boat gets to Beacon. That's where my friend Patterson will join the party. And make dining reservations for any time after that."

"You bet, chief." Dad strolls down the deck and into the cabin —*strolls*, Eddie thinks, as if he's having a relaxed time. His dad feels watched, worries about spilling the coffee on the long carry up from the downstairs dining room. Poor Pop—playing the role of a "good-time Charlie," his mother's dig at Dad for taking this weekend jaunt. She doesn't mean he *is* a "good-time Charlie." She means he doesn't have it in him. Who's he think he's fooling?

"You're one smart boy," Mr. Stone drawls out of the blue. "Ya know how I know that?"

"No, sir."

"Well, first of all," Stone says, hand on Eddie's shoulder, "cause your dad is goddamn proud of you. You know what he says? 'I may be a bum,' he says to me, 'but my boy is gonna make something of himself.' You gonna make something of yourself, Eddie?"

Eddie doesn't answer. "Eddie?"

"My dad is no bum, sir."

"You bet he's not. Glad you stick up for your dad. Hey! Sure! He's my right-hand guy. My top appliance salesman, month after month. He's a well-liked guy. Why you think I'm taking him on this little adventure? Hey—first time you're gonna gamble?"

"I guess so." He wishes Stone would leave him alone. The worst thing is, Stone sounds just like Mom. "*You're* not going to be a bum all your life," she says to him.

Eddie turns away, leans over the rail and takes a snapshot of the river swirling in eddies against the boat steaming against the current, takes another of a smokestack against the sky. Hot day, cool river breezes. How could a picture, even if he had a great camera, catch the whoosh of air gusts and the smell of the Hudson?

"Gin rummy don't count," Mr. Stone says. "I bet you never even seen a horse race." He stretches and yawns like a great lion, waves his fedora to cool off. "Hey—how you like that little tart back there?" he says out of the corner of his mouth—"the one who wouldn't give me the time of day? Imagine!—a bimbo like that?" Mr. Stone laughs an octave lower than his ordinary voice and gets Eddie to laugh. "Stick with me, Eddie. Gonna make hay this weekend. I got plans for you." Stone pats his shoulder, feels his muscles, paws him. Eddie hates it.

Eddie has no idea what Stone's talking about, but he laughs and says, "Yes, *sir*," and closes up the camera. Eddie also hates it when he feels like a fake. He knows how to make himself attractive to adults. All he wants is to slip away and prowl the ship. He's never been on a ship before. He likes the way the iron deck echoes under their feet.

In just a few years, crammed into a troop ship, worried about U-boats, seeing himself burning and drowning in the Atlantic, he'll remember this trip up the Hudson. He'll close his eyes and pretend the GIs are going up to the races in Saratoga, pretend he's looking forward to a weekend full of excitement.

Sid Stone points at Eddie's camera. "Say—how about taking my picture?" Stone stands against the rail and poses, lifting hat from black hair, tilting up his chin in lofty contemplation. Eddie hates being forced into making a picture that's a fake, a fake because the subject is mugging, but he turns the camera on him and carelessly goes click just as Dad appears on deck with two cups of coffee, liquid vibrating to the hum of the engines, cups held in a cardboard frame.

"Here you are, chief," Dad says, handing him his cup.

"Coffee's almost cold," Stone says. "Jesus Christ."

Eddie walks away and leans on a capstan. The bastard! He'd love to accidentally shove the "Big Guy" over the rail and into the river. When Stone goes off to the john, Dad comes over and wraps an arm around Eddie's shoulder. He whispers to Eddie, *whispers* though Stone's nowhere around, "That's how he is, the Big Guy. Sometimes he gets cranky—but then he'll come along and make it up to you."

Eddie shrugs. "Mom's right. I wish you didn't have to work for a four-flusher like that."

"Hey, just look at this." Dad holds up his wrist. On a fat leather strap, a new wrist watch. "Big Guy gave me a stop watch for the track. See?" He presses a steel button and, hunching his shoulders, follows with the forefinger of his other hand an imaginary horse running alongside the ship. "Look at him go, ladies and gents, he's heading for a record for the mile and two furlongs. . . ." He clicks the stopwatch. "Two minutes thirty-nine seconds!"

"And on a very wet track," Eddie laughs, pointing at the Hudson.

"Some snazzy watch, huh?"

"Sure, Dad. Snazzy. Absolutely." Now Eddie slips away and walks the decks, loving the cool winds blowing off the river. Just grinding no meat is a big plus today. Mom should be with us. For his mom, he takes a few pictures of the wooded shore, the cabins and decks, from the prow of the boat.

At Beacon, Stone spots Mr. J. Carter Patterson on the dock and waves. Patterson, a vice-president at GE, will catch the ride in the Caddy from Albany with them. He's a tall drink of water with the water wrung out, *that* dry and skinny—long-faced, short graying hair pasted down, in blazer and creased white ducks. They meet on the lower deck; Stone pats his shoulder. "I hope you're hungry, Carter."

"Oh, satisfactorily." He tilts his panama hat back to open his face, lined, narrow, to the sun.

Stone tugs Eddie's sleeve. "Later on," he whispers, "maybe you can take a snapshot of the two of us." To Patterson—"It's a very special thing you can take off a weekend like this."

Eddie notices that Stone's voice has changed, just as his father's voice changed when Stone came on the scene. Now Stone, the "Big Guy," sounds subdued, more like a radio announcer than a sport. All day Eddie's been seeing his father pretend he's a big shot like Stone; now here's Stone's pretending he's a cool customer like J. Carter Patterson.

"You know," Patterson says, "once every year I go up to Saratoga for the races, Sidney."

They follow Stone into the main saloon, with its paneled walls, its big rubber plants and palms, oversized wicker chairs and ceiling fans, and into the dining room, where a maître d' in a white coat finds Stone's name and seats them at one end of a long table—white cloth and good, heavy tableware. The riveted porthole windows even have white curtains.

Stone slips the man a couple of bills. "Pictures of George Washington for you, my man."

A young family takes up the other end of the table. "Now, what I *don't* like," Stone says out of the corner of his mouth, "is this eating like pigs at a trough, same table with the riffraff."

J. Carter Patterson lifts a big menu card in front of his face.

"Mr. Patterson here," Stone says to Dad, "heads a whole division for GE. That's how we met. Right, Carter?"

J. Carter Patterson smiles a thin-lipped smile above the menu. "That's right. We make what you boys sell. Among other things. But right now, Sidney, I'm more interested in the horses. And the Yankees. Seven and a half games in front, am I right? Pennant race is all sewed up, isn't it, Eddie?"

"But your GE is some concern," Stone says. "Some concern. A corporation for the future. I wish there was a way to. . . ." Stone holds his hands around two imaginary balls and locks his fingertips together. "You know—GE and . . . Stone Furniture and Appliance."

Eddie sees his father is embarrassed for Stone. Eddie's plain amused, watching Stone dig a pit to fall into.

"Well, we're doing a bit of all right again," Patterson says. "Times like this, a time of preparation. Now, nobody wants a war," Patterson says. "Frankly, I see Germany as a buffer against the Bolsheviks. In a way it's doing our job for us. Still, it's profitable—you can imagine: gearing up for war against Hitler does wonders for GE."

"Another war?" Dad says. "Geez. I guess we know too much what modern war is like."

Eddie gets butterflies in his stomach as he remembers pictures of trench warfare and stories his father has told of the Great War. In 1918 Dad's brother Bernie was permanently damaged—his lungs—in a gas attack. Dad's whole machine-gun battalion was wiped out; only a broken leg from a division football game kept Dad from going overseas. Eddie has had nightmares of hiding in a shell crater, dodging bullets, knowing he's about to die. And there's a man Eddie keeps seeing on Columbus Avenue, a man with no nose, a white silk handkerchief shrouding the center of his face.

Eddie is to remember that handkerchief man and this conversation a few years later, December of 1944, in the Ardennes Forest in Belgium, trees crashing around him, their trunks smashed by artillery that's trapped the unit he's been assigned to as a photographer. A falling limb will break his collar bone and smash his camera, and lying in pain in deep snow, waiting for a medic and a needle, he will curse Hitler—but also J. Carter Patterson and GE for making a profit in the war, though he knows it's not their fault.

From the dock at Albany they take a waiting taxi to the railroad station. Eddie goes with his dad to find the big Caddy. His dad keeps wiping the sweat off his face with a crumpled handkerchief. "What if it's not here?" he says.

"It'll be here, Dad."

And there it is, in the parking lot beside the station, black like almost all cars, but Simonized to a deep gloss, no nicks or smudges in the glossy black. Dad checks the whitewall tires. Standing on the running board, he straightens the rearview mirror that sits atop the spare in its shiny case over the fender on the passenger side, and, adjusting the driver's seat, warms up the engine, loving the throaty purr of the sixteen cylinders. Dad grins at Eddie, revs the engine just for the pleasure of it. Handing the attendant a ticket, he eases the Caddy out of the lot to the front of the station, where Eddie hops out, opens the trunk, and puts away the banged-up suitcase he's sharing with his father, Mr. Patterson's light, golden-leather overnight bag, and Mr. Stone's heavy mahogany-leather cases.

Eddie sits up front with his dad; the others take the back. Mr. Patterson sits up straight and watches the scenery, his arms folded over his thin chest. Stone sprawls, his arms spread over the back of the leather seat—to express, Eddie thinks, his leisurely ownership of the car. Not wanting to spoil the weekend, Eddie keeps his mind on the winged stainless-steel goddess leaning into the wind from the hood, and beyond her, the green hills of upper New York State.

Creeping the last twenty miles behind a truck transporting live chickens, with Stone nagging Dad to "pass the son of a bitch already"—though the road's too curved for passing—they roll into Saratoga late and check in to the gigantic Grand Union on Broadway. It's almost dark, but the main hotel restaurant is open. Eddie and his father share a cramped room on the top floor. Once servants' quarters. To get there they have to take the elevator to the floor below and walk the rest of the way. Stone, of course, has a big room on the third floor with a fancy satin spread on the oversized bed. Heavy, polished furniture fills the high-ceilinged space. Eddie knows this because he and his dad carried Stone's bags from the car. Up in their own room, his dad says, "Well, this is okay. Don't tell mom. She'll say 'I told you so.'"

"Aw, our room's fine. Old fashioned, a little small, but we're not paying for it."

"You bet. And dinner's on the Big Guy."

They unpack and dress up for dinner. Last week Mom took him downtown and bought him clothes. "If you're going to travel with that Steinberg, I'm not going to have you looking shabby." So he's wearing a new shirt, tie, and seersucker summer suit. For his mom, these are his young-lawyer or young-doctor clothes, harbingers of a future by which he can redeem her life. They wait downstairs for Stone and Patterson in the huge, pretentious lobby with its great chandelier.

"Imagine if all that crystal dropped on some poor son of a gun?" his father says.

Eddie spots a really pretty girl, blonde, perfect, coming out of the dining room with her family. And she notices him, too—he can tell. She must think he's a rich kid with a rich father. She must imagine that, in his house, fights about money never explode. He tries, in the way he carries himself, in the way he smiles at her, to act the part.

Dinner is "admirable," says Mr. Patterson. Well, Eddie thinks, at twelve dollars a plate—more than twice what he makes working all day in the butcher shop—it should be. Stone signs the tab. "Very nice of you, Sidney," Mr. Patterson says. "I'll take care of breakfast at the track—we'll see the morning workout and eat a big, Southern breakfast near the paddocks. I'll see you fellows in the morning. Got to get to bed on the early side if we're going to be at the track by six."

"I've heard about those track breakfasts, Carter. Quite a spread, huh?"

"Believe me. There's nothing like it. Before the crowds gather. You see horses plunging through the mist of a morning," he says this—almost, Eddie thinks, sings it—while his fingers draw vague pictures in the imaginary, mist-filled air. Funny. The man sure doesn't look poetic. Looks sculpted out of a block of wood. "I can get us in," J. Carter Patterson says. "And let me tell you—you can learn quite a bit about performance watching the horses work out."

"Great. Great. Here I thought we were gonna go on the town tonight," Stone says, looking up at Patterson, pouting a little. "Well, as for me, I know I'm heading for the betting tables after dinner. What about you, Marty?"

"Oh, Mr. Stone, Sid, frankly, I hate to lose."

"Lose? Why talk like a loser? Am I right, Carter? Say, I'll tell you what, Marty. You stay here in the hotel. I'll take Eddie with me. I promised the kid. How about it, Eddie?"

"No, thanks, Mr. Stone. I'm bushed."

They watch Stone stride off alone to conquer Saratoga Springs. Then Eddie and his father stroll Broadway. Eddie has walked into a Katharine Hepburn movie. There are groups of well-dressed summer people everywhere on the wide, leafy streets, women in high heels, men in white ascots at the throat, white silk glowing against the black of tuxedos under the streetlights and the lights of the hotels and bars. They're familiar from the movies—gangster movies, society comedies. Yet it's as if his camera-eye tells him the truth: nobody here is a gangster; nobody is high society.

Maybe everybody is looking for real gangsters and real high society.

"Dad? Work for Stone? I'd rather work in the butcher shop. He isn't gonna buy me."

And his father sings out a sigh. "You mean the way he's bought me."

"I didn't say that, Dad."

"No, it's your mother says that. But he's a special type of personality, Eddie. He can't help being pushy. It's . . . the best he can do. Say!—look over there at that lady coming up the steps. See? Now, is that classy? She could be in the movies. Couldn't she? No offense to your mother, Eddie, I'm just observing. She looks like— you know—a gardenia. That dress of hers, thin as pink tissue paper. Can't you see her in a movie with Clark Gable? Tell you what, Eddie. Let's slug down a glass of mineral water for our digestion and get us the hell to bed."

Next day, Saturday, is looking to be a scorcher. Eddie's glad to be getting up in the cool of the morning, and yes, Patterson is right, as the sun rises there's mist, mist diffusing the sunrise, particularly beautiful when you watch an exercise boy up on a lone horse loping around the track, seeming to float through the mist rising from the dirt. They watch the horses through giant field glasses Mr. Stone and Mr. Patterson have brought along. Eddie takes a couple of pictures as homage to what he sees, but with the Kodak he doesn't have a chance of catching that early sun glowing through the dust and mist. If there's one thing in the world Eddie wishes for, it's a Leica.

How big the horses are! They're not like the horses in Central Park. He doesn't know what he's supposed to look at, why some of the men suddenly buzz with talk at the way a horse moves. There are men with stopwatches. He's saved twenty dollars to bet on the races. He figures he'll lose most of it. It'll be worth it for the fun of having a horse to cheer on. So he eyes each horse, trying to find the ones that look beautiful. But they all look beautiful to him. When they come close, he snaps pictures that he knows can't be worthy of the horses.

They stand at the rail. Mr. Stone and Mr. Patterson hold field glasses. "That bay is Flight Command," Mr. Patterson says. "He won last week when Andy K was disqualified. You must have read the story?"

"Oh, sure, sure," Mr. Stone says.

Six thirty: Breakfast is gigantic. At some tables the men have ordered steaks. For most, for themselves, it's ham, eggs, and grits or potatoes, served by black waiters on great round tables set on a grassy floor under a yellow and white striped tent. Eddie notices that the roof over the empty grandstand rises to a series of peaks that themselves look like tents. It kind of reminds him of a Technicolor movie, knights jousting in behalf of maidens. "That's Eight-thirty," Mr. Patterson says, putting down his glasses. "We may see Fighting Fox today."

"Say! What do you know for today's races?" Stone asks. "Any inside scoop?"

"Not a great deal," says Mr. Patterson, who drops his eyes to his platter.

Mr. Stone develops a furrow between his brows. "You boys should have come along last night. I made some easy pickings at the blackjack tables."

"How much did you win, Sid?" Eddie's father asks.

"Puh-lenty." Then, when Patterson doesn't look up, he says, "Say. Next week is the sale of yearlings, Carter."

"Mmm. Why don't you take all those winnings, Stone, and buy yourself a colt?"

"Funny man."

After breakfast they wander through the paddock to the roofed rows of stalls, the smell of horses strong. A small Negro is lugging an enormous sack of hay—clean hay? Mucked hay? It's twice the man's size. A boy Eddie's age is mucking out a stall. Eddie wishes he were wearing clothes he didn't have to keep clean, shoes he didn't have to keep out of horse droppings. Not that it's filthy back here; it's surprisingly clean. And not that he's dressed up, but he's got only this one pair of slacks. The boy in the stall—Eddie'd like to meet him. What he'd really like is to get away from the phonies—and even from his father, who keeps reading the names of horses in the sixth race, as if saying the names makes him seem to know something.

At ten, the management clears spectators from the track, and they drive back to town. Stone points out the night club, closed till evening, owned by Arnold Rothstein, "the guy Dewey just sent to the hoosegow," Stone says. "And that place with the white columns—a gambling joint, a big one—they say it's owned by Meyer Lansky. It's a peculiar thing, isn't it, Carter, the way these society types mix with gangsters up here?"

J. Carter Patterson grunts in reply; he has the *Daily Racing Form* open, and he's making notes in pencil in a little notebook. Stone shakes his head. As they get out at the hotel, Stone puts a hand over his mouth and whispers to Eddie, "Some personality, that candy-ass."

"Dad? You going to bet this afternoon?" Eddie asks when they're alone, scrubbing down the Caddy. Eddie has borrowed a pail, sponge, and water from the hotel kitchen, and towels from their own bathroom, and as he sponges off the dust, his father rubs back the shine.

"Oh, sure I'll bet. You want to, I'll give you a few bucks."

"That's okay. I brought some from my savings. Just enough to have some fun. What the hell, right Dad? I'll try to keep a couple of bucks for every race."

"I'm gonna bet with Sid Stone. He knows horses. Last year, he won a bundle."

They drive back to the track in time for the first race. News on the radio—diplomatic appeals to Hitler. Eddie sees in mind's eye the letters his father wrote at the kitchen table for his mom's cousins in Berlin. Letter after letter to Immigration and members of Congress offering to vouch for the cousins if they're given a visa. "You see?" his mom says. "See what happens when you pretend you're not a Jew? They thought it was different for them. They're rich, they're cultured. Then along comes a Hitler."

Stone grumbles about the dust swirling up from the tires of the long line of cars up ahead. "But after all, what's a little dust?" Patterson says. "Comes off with a hose. It's a fine automobile Cadillac makes. I wouldn't have any other."

"Sure. Packard dealer tried to sell me one of their big touring cars. I stick to Cadillac."

They pass another Caddy, and looking over, Eddie spots the pretty girl from last night. He leans out of the window as their car passes, but he can't catch her eye.

At the paddock they lean on the rail watching the thoroughbreds circle, ridden or led by a trainer on another horse. Eddie watches Patterson's eyes, Patterson's pencil, makes note in his own *Racing Form* of a horse to try. This is the last year the bookmakers still take bets with boards and slips of paper. Next year the mechanical pari-mutuel machines take over. They make their bets by the paddock and go back to their seats close to the rail. The stands are crammed with men in open white shirts, women in pastels. Eddie, using Patterson's eyes as his guide, has bet five dollars on Shangay Lily. Stone and his father have bet on Redlin, the favorite. Patterson doesn't discuss his bet.

Eddie's surprised how long it takes to get the horses closed into the starting gate. Now the bell and an explosion of dust, though the track has just been sprinkled. Eddie wishes he were higher up, where he could see what's what. The race is announced by a man up above the stands, but over the screams and roars of the crowd it's hard to make out anything. He sees the horses press together on the turn away from him, then string out along the back stretch and into the curve. They're near the finish line, and he's on his feet screaming, "Shangay Lily! Shangay Lily!" though he doesn't know for certain which horse that is. Patterson, he notices from the corner of his eye, is silent. Stone is opening and closing his mouth as if biting air, hunching forward, punching his palm, moving his shoulders in a kind of body English, then slumps back as Shangay Lily crosses the line a length and a half ahead. Eddie turns away to grin.

By the end of the afternoon, Eddie has won a few bets and lost a few bets. He's surprised—he's come out thirty dollars ahead. He sees Patterson tearing up his betting slip from the last race. "I've done all right this afternoon," Patterson says as they walk to the parking lot.

"What the hell," Stone says. "I didn't do so bad myself. The real gambling we'll try tonight at the Piping Rock. Are you with me?"

"You bet, Sid," Dad says. "I've still got half what I brought to lose."

"Let's see how I feel after dinner," Patterson says.

"Damn dust," Stone says. He brushes the car with a handkerchief. "Marty, you think you can wash this goddamn car down for me?"

"Sure. Sure. Eddie and I did it this morning. I don't mind."

"I noticed. I noticed. Nice. That's exactly why the damn dust from the road bugged me. Well, I guess you got a good steak coming. And for you, Eddie, I got a little special surprise, don't you worry. And Carter, well, you can just be an old stick-in-the-mud if you want."

Eddie lies on his bed reading a book of stories by Ring Lardner he got as a gift for his seventeenth birthday. His dad is dozing in a chair by the window, newspaper in lap. His face is slack and puffy; he doesn't need to prove anything. The newspaper covers his lap like a skirt.

Eddie feels for him. Why does it hit him now? Maybe because he's awake and watching over his father? He goes for his camera, sets up a photograph using light from the window and dragging a floor lamp over so the shadows on his dad's face won't be too severe. With a suitcase on end as tripod, he takes a few pictures. The chair and man framed in the window; then a picture of his father's head and chest; finally, he goes as close to his father's face as the camera permits without blur. What can he do with these pictures? Will his dad want a picture of himself sleeping in a chair?

Eddie feels tears welling up, and as he returns the lamp to its place, he imagines some day when his father will be old, an old guy, and he'll be able to say, *Dad, I'm going to take good care of you. I know how you like the beach. We're going to take a great vacation this year. We'll rent a fabulous place right on the ocean . . .*

. . . It never happens. The day that the unit he's assigned to as a photographer—the same day that unit enters Dachau—his father, on the other side of the ocean, is struck by a heart attack and drops like a tree. *Like a tree*, his mother will say. *He knew nothing, the good soul. He asked me what we were having for dinner. That's all. And then he fell.*

Before the call that day from his mother, he will be shaking, quivering as if he had a fever, unable to eat, from too much seeing, photographing all day piles of the dead, bulldozed stacks of ragged clothing, the living hanging by their fingers from the wire. Dachau wasn't technically a "death camp" like Auschwitz. Some of the half-dead in their striped uniforms are fit enough to grin and wave at the camera. But those bare skulls with big ears, eyes staring: he is ashamed to look, let alone photograph. It's real—a true thing—but seems obscene.

The captain keeps pointing at him. "Rubin—for Chrissakes we need a record. That's your job, Rubin." All day he records Dachau. *Arbeit Macht Frei*—the letters in wrought iron. When soldiers, full of what they've seen, start massacring SS-Waffen troops, maybe fifty of them, soldiers with the death-head insignias who surrendered in the adjoining camp, that same captain waves him off. Eddie turns his camera on Americans unloading corpses from cattle cars, where prisoners had been locked in without food or water.

So his father's death will always be wrapped in those dead and those skeletal survivors, in the photographs he printed and sent out by courier. Maybe, he thinks, his rich cousins are somewhere in those photographs, among the living or the dead. They're real to him now.

After dinner, they stroll in the late glow of sun through the leafy trees that line the street. Under the colonnades at the Grand Union and the United States, little tables are set, and casually dressed couples and foursomes are drinking. A foreign open touring car, a man in a tweed hat driving alone, passes them, and they all follow it with their eyes. J. Carter Patterson seems almost mellow this evening, Eddie notices, breathing deeply, his hands linked behind his back as if he were in a museum. But Sid Stone wants to firm up plans. "Later on, we can drive out to the Lakeside House or over to the Piping Rock. What d'ya say? I buy you a drink, Carter?"

No one says anything. Eddie catches Stone's angry look—eyes narrowed, mouth clenched. They keep walking.

For Eddie things are *real* or *not real*. The horses raising dust as the riders lean into the turns, that's real. That's what he wants to turn into photos. Stone, his gambling, his swagger, they're unreal. Eddie would just as soon stay out of the gambling places tonight. Why? Because it's going to turn his dad unreal.

"First," Stone says, not giving up, looking at his watch, "there's this little saloon from Prohibition days—it's just around the corner. It's got character, you know what I mean?"

"Sure, Sid, sure," Dad says to fill the void. "Like the old saloons in New York."

"Exactly."

"Well. One drink," Mr. Patterson says.

It's a long bar, brass and dark wood glowing. Standing with one foot up on the rail, they look at themselves over the bottles in a mirror that stretches the length of the bar. It's early. The place is still pretty empty—a group of men, another, a couple of frothy young ladies in colorful, ankle-length dresses. Stone waves his fingers, and one of the ladies laughs and comes over. "Oh, it's Mr. Stone. I *do* remember you from last year, Mr. Stone."

Eddie realizes that Stone is not at all surprised, though he pretends to be. Which means this meeting was prearranged. Stone shakes her hand, then pulls her close. Eddie, next to him, smells her perfume. Stone whispers in her ear, not a real whisper—everyone is supposed to hear him: "We're four very lonely guys, Nancy. Four boys out on the town, and I wonder if you know anyone. . . ."

"Well, Mr. Stone, you know, it's entirely possible. . . ."

Patterson drinks down his whiskey in one gulp. He draws back from the bar, lifts his palms to Stone and spreads them out as if he were a mime describing a wall or a priest keeping off the devil. "I'm afraid this ends our evening, Stone. I thought you were a married man."

"Not me. Once upon a time, Carter. Not anymore."

"Well, Stone, I am. A married man. And Eddie, here—well, Eddie is a *boy*. Perhaps to you that's inconsequential—"

"Not at all. Not at all. But say, it's not like that, is it, Nancy?"

"Well, Mr. Stone, it certainly doesn't have to be."

"Okay, Carter. Then I'll be seeing you. How about you, Marty? Are you game?"

"Game? What game do you mean, Sid?"

"And the boy here." Stone's smile fades, but his eyes stay narrow. "Say! I'm trying to give folks a treat. I just want to give Eddie a little gift he'll remember."

Eddie sucks a deep breath. He guesses he'll have to speak up for himself this time, and he's about to when Dad puts an arm around his shoulders and backs away from the bar.

"Sid? Jesus, Sid. I keep defending you, Sid. But this is the limit," his father says. "You're embarrassing Eddie here, you're embarrassing me. And I'll tell you what—you're embarrassing a gentleman you want to impress. Why you doing that?"

"I 'want to impress'? Who? You mean *this* fine Waspy gentleman? You're wrong, Marty. I am who I am. You can take it or leave it. It's been pretty obvious all day that Mr. Patterson here is turning up his nose. Well, that's okay with me, Carter."

Patterson looks at his watch and yawns—"I believe it's time to get back to the hotel and call home." He nods to Eddie and his father, and he's gone.

Dad turns. The girl, too, seeing the way the wind lies, she's gone—back to her friend at the other end of the bar. They start laughing. Stone is paying the tab. "All right, Marty. I'll see you tomorrow for the ride back to Albany."

"Thanks for the offer. We can get back on our own, right Eddie? And I guess you know how to drive, Sid, don't you?"

In the darkness outside, his father tilts his head at him, questioning. "I know it's weird," Eddie says. "I can't stand the guy, but now I can't help feeling bad for him. He tries so hard."

"We're through, me and that son of a bitch. Can you imagine—a cheap trick like that? Let me tell you, Eddie—he didn't do that for you. He did it to put me into a lousy position. I'm never gonna forget it."

"Dad? Neither is Stone."

"I know," his father says, gloomily. "Well to hell with him. Stone. *Steinberg*," his father says. "Steinberg, the phony. Your mom's right. That's who he is, the son of a bitch."

"Dad? Thanks. I mean it. Thanks a lot."

"Sure. What for?" his dad asks, grinning.

He will try to explain *what for* to the young woman in Heidelberg when he shares her big iron bed with its soft, down featherbed. Autumn of 1945—Eddie will be assigned to Eisenhower's headquarters. He'll try to explain to her why he thanked his father. This will be in her small room with a coal stove, a sublet in a large apartment within a stone building on a court, a building that dates back to the early seventeenth century. The first Shakespeare troupe to tour Germany once stayed here, she'll tell him. Out the window, down the cobbled street, is the Alte Brücke, lit by moonlight.

"Of course," he tells this very young woman who's accepted the simple offer he made in the *wein stube* around the corner, "I was a kid, I was scared. But it wasn't that. It was Dad's courage, *mut*, precisely —*genau, verstehen?*—because Dad *wasn't* a brave guy, because he always bowed down to his boss." *Boss* he mugs by looking up, lifting a fist up over their heads. "The Big Guy. But not this time."

This girl is very lean. He strokes her hip. Beautiful, beautiful— but maybe, he thinks, lean because she hasn't had enough to eat. He'll offer to go to the PX for her. Then he wonders what she *knew* these past few years—and her beauty will be spoiled. He wonders this all the time, all the damn time. He keeps seeing that pile of skeletons and those near-skeletons, their fingers hooked into the steel-wire fence. They're all eager to reassure him, these Germans. When he says, "I'm Jewish. You understand?"—they frown and tell him about the Jews they helped save or the Jews who were their dear friends. Everyone he meets. Phonies! It puts the kibosh on getting to know people.

But he wants her to understand, because he's still grieving for his father. There's so much to tell Dad, and now he'll never see him. He thinks back about Saratoga and the races and the gutsy way his father stood up for him, took a chance on losing his job. "And he *did* lose it," he tells her. "He lost his job for me. Stone

found a way to get rid of him"—Eddie makes a gesture of dismissal
—"a couple of months later. We all knew why. Mom was happy
about it. She said it was the best thing that could have happened.
My dad would shrug and blush—face turn red, *rot*, *farshtaist?*—
because for once she was proud of him. And *I* was proud of him.
I loved the guy a lot."

He's glad it's dark in the little room in Heidelberg so the girl
can't see his eyes.

Sunday morning Eddie and his father wake up late, and in the
courtyard of the Grand Union they eat sausages and eggs and look
over the formal gardens—soak it in, knowing Stone will be paying
and they can't accept anything more from him nor pay for this
fancy place themselves. They'll take the train down to the city later
this morning.

J. Carter Patterson spies them, lifts a finger, and comes over.

"Good morning, good morning, Mr. Patterson. Sit with us?"

"I've eaten, Mr. Rubin. But just for a minute, I shall." A waiter
brings a silver service, coffee, cream and sugar. He smiles. "Well.
That was quite enough vulgarity for one weekend, wasn't it?" Patterson fixes himself a cup of coffee and relaxes. "That employer of
yours! I was *very* pleased you walked out on him last night. Now
you, Mr. Rubin, you're of the Jewish persuasion, am I correct? And
that's fine with me. Absolutely fine. I respect a fine Jewish gentleman. But this *Stone?*" Patterson lifts a teaching forefinger. "You
can always spot the deception."

Now his father shocks Eddie. It's something he will always remember, the way his father answers Patterson. If he hadn't stood
up to Stone the night before, maybe he'd never have answered Patterson this morning. On that night in Heidelberg six years later,
Eddie will try to explain it to the girl who shares his bed, but she
doesn't get it. She shakes her head and closes her eyes and yawns,
and her golden hair spreads over the white pillow. He stops trying; he stops thinking; he caresses her. He tries to forget what she
knew, and when.

"I know you mean well, Mr. Patterson," Dad says, "but I think you never ought to say you respect a 'fine Jewish gentleman.' I mean. I mean you should say you respect a *gentleman*. See what I mean?" His father puts down knife and fork and waves a forefinger. "I can't help remembering a saying of my father's. He used to warn me: 'A kike,' he'd say, 'a kike is a *Jewish gentleman* who's just left the room.'"

The smile on Mr. Patterson's face fades. "Well. Perhaps I misspoke," he says. "I certainly didn't mean anything by it. If you knew me better . . . Very nice meeting you both." He touches the brim of his Panama straw hat and walks away.

"A nice Christian gentleman," Dad says and, grinning, pokes Eddie. "We better get a move on. Train leaves at eleven."

"We could take a later train, Dad—go to the races by ourselves. I mean—we're here."

"I'm not all that much of a gambler, Eddie."

"Okay, Dad. Me neither."

Back in New York after the war, Eddie will be walking along Madison Avenue, still in uniform because the uniform looks better than any of his old civilian clothes. He's hunting a job. And whom does he see?—J. Carter Patterson, who spots him, too. Eddie remembers his father's crack about Christian gentlemen, and he almost slips away. But is that fair? Patterson was jake. So Eddie smiles a broad smile, and Patterson doffs his fedora in return.

"Yes," he says. "I remember you and your father just before the war."

"That's right, Mr. Patterson. I'm Eddie Rubin. My father, Marty, he died almost a year ago."

"I'm sorry to hear that. I remember you both. I liked you both. That was the weekend with that amazing—" He shrugs, waves his fingers searching for the name. Eddie doesn't prompt him, doesn't want to talk about Sid Stone. "So—you made master sergeant. Well, well. Very impressive. Are you still in the army, soldier?"

"For another month. I'm on separation leave. I'm looking for a job."

"I see. And what did you do over there?"

Eddie's a little embarrassed. "I carried a camera, not usually a rifle. Now I'm looking for a job in photography. Maybe in journalism."

J. Carter Patterson lights up. He takes a card from his wallet, scribbles something on the back, hands the card to Eddie. "You give this man a call. You give him a call," he says, tapping his card. "He's at the *Journal-American*."

And this is the way Eddie's career in journalism will get started. From the *Journal-American* he'll go to the *Post*, from the *Post* to *Newsweek*. Even after he marries he'll take pictures everywhere. He'll cover Korea. He'll cover Vietnam. He'll cover Martin Luther King in Memphis.

But he'll never forget that day they liberated Dachau. Those pictures never leave him—a vision of skin and bones, elbows and knees sticking up toward life as if they belonged to drowning swimmers. They're somehow embedded in all the photographs he's ever taken. If that weekend in Saratoga taught him something about fakery, Dachau made fakery shameful and impossible. "The thing I first liked about you," the woman who becomes his wife will tell him, "is how honest you are. Like your photographs. You just tell the truth."

In the late seventies, their kids grown, he and Ellen will drive up the Thruway to Saratoga, where he'll take pictures for a photographic essay in *National Geographic*. The old Grand Union Hotel is closed. Saratoga's a city, no longer a town. Its souvenirs and shops *imitate* prewar, elegant Saratoga. So the truth of the pictures from this visit is the truth of falsity. That's something he's learned, something he didn't know the last time he was here—to find the truth within falsity, the truth of falsity. That picture of a mugging Mr. Stone, if he found it among his old photos, would tell its own peculiar truth.

He tells Ellen about the weekend that changed his father's life and, in the long run, his own. "Last time I was here, everyone was putting on the dog. I saw it so plain. I swore I'd never live that way. We came home by train. We ate in the dining car. 'Like a couple of swells,' Dad said. Next day I went back to work at the butcher shop."

On the train going home, Eddie sits next to Dad, hand on his shoulder. Today, they're a couple of pals, watching the Hudson go by. Once they pass a Hudson River Day Line boat on its way to New York. Eddie notices that Dad's no longer wearing that watch Stone gave him. He never wears it again. Eddie finds the watch in the back of a drawer when he comes back to New York after the war and is looking through his father's things. Now, on the train ride home, Dad seems relieved, having told off that sonofabitch. He seems bigger, grander.

"Eddie, m'boy," he says, almost singing the words, "I could wear me a snazzy Panama hat, I could put on the most gorgeous linen trousers in the whole world, I could learn all about the horses—it won't do me any good. No way I'm ever gonna be an American sport."

Eddie grabs his father around the shoulder. His father's face is hot as always. From inches away he feels the heat, sees graying prickles of unshaven beard. He wants to whisper something wonderful but can't get the words out. He rubs his knuckles over his dad's rough cheek.

Clayton, born and raised in New York City, taught modern literature and fiction writing as professor and then professor emeritus at the University of Massachusetts, Amherst, and as Visiting Professor at Mt. Holyoke College and Hampshire College. He lives with his wife in western Massachusetts and Cape Cod.